BRANNA

a slater brothers novella

NEW YORK TIMES & USA TODAY BESTSELLING AUTHOR

L. A. CASEY

Branna
a slater brothers novella
Copyright © 2017 by L.A. Casey
Published by L.A. Casey
www.lacaseyauthor.com

Branna / L.A. Casey – 1st ed.
ISBN-13: 978-1543085815 | ISBN-10: 1543085814

ALSO BY L.A. CASEY

SLATER BROTHERS SERIES

DOMINIC
BRONAGH
ALEC
KEELA
KANE
AIDEEN
RYDER

STANDALONE NOVELS
FROZEN
UNTIL HARRY

Branna and Ryder lovers—BRANNA is for you guys,
because God knows you've wanted it to release more than me.
:)

TABLE OF CONTENTS

CHAPTER ONE

Having a near-death experience at the hands of a psychopathic lunatic was *not* something I would ever forget but I was doing a damn good job trying. My family, on the other hand, were not. It was constantly on their minds and wasn't something they could just sweep under the carpet. I understood that and, while I loved their attentiveness and concern for my mental health, I was a *hair* away from admitting myself into an asylum to get away from the overbearing freaks.

I hated thinking that because it made me sound ungrateful. I wasn't ungrateful. I *really* got it. I got where they were coming from. When I was kidnapped five months ago and put through the wringer by Big Phil—an American arsehole who was now six feet under—my family could only be expected to hover. If they didn't constantly surround me, I could have possibly dealt with my situation differently. Even though I refused to give the scumbag any power over me, even in death, I appreciated my family being there as a backbone for me in case I did break.

I didn't, though.

Luckily, I kept my shit together and didn't let Big Phil in. *Sometimes,* I had the occasional night terror where I would dream of what happened and wake up in a cold sweat, but it never made me fear falling asleep. The Health Board that oversaw the maternity hospital

I worked at appointed me to see a therapist that had to sign off on whether I was mentally stable enough to continue working. I was originally signed on for six sessions with her, but that rolled into twenty before she was convinced I was mentally okay. She signed off on me—thank God—and she admitted to being surprised that I wasn't more of a wreck after what I had been through. The only reason I could think as to why I wasn't *totally* unstable was because my mind and heart had been put through way worse when I spent a year and a half being at my lowest point over Ryder Slater.

He was a unique man with a *very* unique past. I would usually only read about the things he and his four brothers had been through in books or see on films. Getting involved with him wasn't scary; I fell in love with him so fast that it made my head spin, but it clouded my senses and judgment. Because of that, I allowed myself to become close to a person who had enemies and instantly became a prime target for those enemies.

My little sister, Bronagh, found her own way to Ryder's younger brother, Dominic. My best friend, Aideen Collins, got tied up with Ryder's other brother, Kane. Aideen's best friend, Keela Daley, got tangled up with Ryder's *other* brother, Alec. And Bronagh's best friend, Alannah Ryan, was briefly involved with the youngest of the Slater brothers—Damien. That association put them all at risk.

Literally *all* of them.

When my sister was eighteen, she was kidnapped by a disgusting excuse for a human being named Marco Miles who wanted to use her as a bargaining chip to keep the brothers under his thumb—Damien and Alannah were also taken as insurance. Damien remembered everything that happened, but Alannah had no clue other than she "fainted," and we decided to keep it that way. She was pure, and we weren't sure if she could handle the brothers' past, and what she was involved in, without breaking down. Keela was taken by the *same* arsehole a few years later in a bid to get revenge on the brothers for destroying his empire. Nearly two years ago, Aideen was attacked and almost burned alive while she was pregnant with her son,

Jax, because *another* scumbag named Big Phil wanted revenge on Kane for killing his paedophile son many years ago. That same son of a bitch abducted me a few months ago to draw Kane out so he could finally get the revenge he had always wanted.

All attempts backfired.

You would think after it happening so much that we would kind of get used to the idea of someone in our circle being kidnapped and tortured, but nope, it was hard to digest each time we found ourselves in a situation like that. The only thing we could be thankful for was that everyone from the brothers' past who had ill will against them were dead, so we didn't have to worry about anything happening to any of us ever again.

Which, let me tell you, was *immensely* relieving.

Because of what we had been through, I understood and validated my family's behaviour. That being said, it was a struggle all the same to deal with because my little sister was possibly the *most* overbearing out of everyone. She was slowly driving me crazy. Ryder, my newly wedded husband, was bad, but he didn't have a patch on Bronagh. She had become my shadow since my attack, but she recently stepped up her game and stuck to me like glue after my surprise wedding and pregnancy announcement three weeks ago.

I was now married to the love of my life and expecting his baby, and this sent Bronagh into full alert. She was constantly in I-will-take-on-God-himself-to-protect-my-sister mode. I couldn't be mad at her for it, even though she *did* sometimes make me question why I didn't file for a restraining order against her. She meant well—that was what I kept repeating to myself whenever the urge to pick the phone and call the Garda arose.

The urge was *dangerously* tempting at the current moment.

"Bee." I chortled as I placed a folded pair of leggings into my suitcase. "You know I'm goin' on me honeymoon, right? That *kind* of means you can't come."

I still couldn't believe I was going on a *real* honeymoon. Ryder surprised me with a wedding, a truly beautiful wedding that was more than I could have ever dreamed of. When I thought about it, and how all of those I loved were involved in it, I still got giddy and checked my left hand for my ring just to make sure it was real and that I didn't just make believe it happened.

I was *really* married to Ryder Slater, and I loved every single second of it.

We were leaving for our little getaway later in the evening, and since I'd worked more shifts than usual over the past month, it meant I left all my packing until the last minute. I wasn't stressed about it. In fact, I wasn't worried about it in the slightest because Ryder and I were going to a cabin deep in a private woodland three hours away, where we wouldn't need much of anything. The package deal Ryder bought was an all-inclusive secluded getaway. The cabin we would be staying in would have enough food and supplies for the two weeks we would be there. It was originally only supposed to be a one-week visit, but Ryder extended it for us to have extra alone time. He even picked some additional goodies, since my appetite and sweet tooth had been growing with each added week into my pregnancy.

I had been daydreaming about it since Ryder told me about the fantasy trip after we got married. We were both constantly surrounded by our family, and people in general, so going somewhere where it was going to be *just* the two of us for two whole weeks had me twisted up in all kind of knots. The *good* kind of knots that my husband would surely spend hours working out with his hands, mouth, and coc—"Branna, are you even *listenin'* to me?"

I jumped when Bronagh's voice cut off my train of thought, and I hoped my guilt didn't show on my face.

I cleared my throat. "Of course."

My sister deadpanned, "What did I just say then?"

Shite.

"Um... you were sayin' that... you... that you should come on the honeymoon with us regardless of what Ryder and everyone else thinks... right?"

My sister raised her brows. "Oh, you were listenin'. Sorry."

I would have thought myself psychic for guessing correctly if I didn't know my sister so well. She had become shockingly predictable over the last few weeks. I knew her every move before she played it, and it helped keep me sane because I knew when she was about to pull something *in*sane.

Like now, I silently grumbled.

"So yeah," Bronagh continued. "I should go. I will stay in me own room with Georgie 'cause I obviously have to bring 'er. We won't bother you both but—"

"No," I cut her off.

She narrowed her eyes at me and said, "Give me *one* good reason why we shouldn't go."

I could have listed millions, but I went with the most important one.

"Because it's me *honeymoon*."

"So?" Bronagh huffed. "We can make it a *family*moon and—"

I cut my sister off with joyous laughter, and it irked her.

"You're actin' the maggot now," she grumbled. "I'm bein' *dead* serious about this."

That was what made it so funny.

"Bee, would you want me to come along on *your* honeymoon?" I asked and smirked knowingly. "Think about it *very* hard now. While you and Dominic are lovin' each other as hard as you possibly could, would you want me in the next room gettin' a play by play of each nip, kiss, slap, and thrust?"

Bronagh's face scrunched up in distaste.

"For God's sake! Why'd you have to go and word it like that?" she asked, and shivered in what I think was disgust.

I loved that we were both adults, but sometimes, I could still gross her out when it came to conversing about sex. It reminded me of our ten-year age gap and that she was still my little sister even though she didn't act like it a lot of the time. She was grown and had a child now, but she was still the annoying brat who touched my stuff growing up, and no one could ever change that. Not even her.

I smiled affectionately. "Because you *know* what you and Dominic would do with all that alone time. It's *exactly* what me and Ryder will be doin'."

She folded her arms across her chest and said nothing further. I waited for her to mull it over in her mind, and when she sighed, I knew she was going to relent and not press the issue any longer.

"Fine." She dramatically threw her arms up in the air. "I give up. Go have wild monkey sex with your husband for two weeks, and I'll hold down the fort here."

I lifted my hand in the air, and she snorted as she raised her arm and slapped her palm against mine.

"Good lookin' out, sis." I winked.

"If you weren't already pregnant," she mused, "you would be by the time you come home."

I simpered. "I know; Ryder is *so* excited that we don't have to use condoms anymore."

Bronagh blinked. "You weren't on birth control *before*?"

I shook my head. "The pill doesn't agree with me, and the bar in me arm gave me constant headaches. Do you remember before the lads came into our lives I'd cry with the pain before I got it removed?"

Concern washed over my sister's face.

"Yeah, that sucked."

I nodded in agreement. "You can say that again."

"So you and Ry have just been usin' johnnies this entire time?" she asked, her eyebrows raised with curiosity.

"Yep."

"I wouldn't have just trusted that. After Dominic and I had sex for the first time and after the whole Marco bullshit, I went on the pill straight away. I was terrified I'd get pregnant 'cause we were goin' at it so much."

My lips quirked. "You can talk about sex with Dominic, but I can't talk about sex with Ryder?"

"You can, but it just freaks me out sometimes."

I chuckled. "I'm only teasin', but yeah, for us, condoms worked. Once or twice, they broke, but Ryder noticed it straight away and changed them or pulled out."

"Change the topic." Bronagh squealed. "*Seriously*."

I gleefully laughed, but quickly shut my mouth when a high-pitched cry sounded from downstairs. My sister sighed and lifted her hands to her breasts as she said, "Georgie's hungry."

We listened and smiled when we heard the cries get louder as heavy footsteps walked up the stairs accompanied by cooing and kissing sounds. Dominic was bringing his daughter up to Bronagh, and he was doing it in typical daddy fashion. When he entered my room, he locked eyes on Bronagh, and for a second, his pupils dilated. I loved when I caught a glimpse of the second he landed his eyes on her. It was as if he got an instant reaction just from seeing her, and was discovering all over again that she was his. I had noticed it back when he looked at her when they were just kids, and his reaction to her hadn't faltered in the slightest over the years.

"Mini Pretty Girl is hungry," he said, his eyes still trained on Bronagh as he swayed Georgie from side to side.

My sister held her arms out with a sigh. "She's *always* hungry."

"There's nothing wrong with that," Dominic said as he crossed the room, and lowered Georgie into her mother's arms.

My niece, who was still fussing, settled when Bronagh opened a small zip on her t-shirt under her left breast exposing her nipple to her daughter only. Georgie instantly latched on and began feeding, though she continued to fuss.

I loved the breastfeeding clothing Dominic had gotten Bronagh. She loved breastfeeding but didn't feel comfortable doing it in public. Before the clothes, she would go somewhere private to feed her daughter, but now, she could feed her anywhere. The pieces were stylish, trendy, and looked completely normal, but around the breast area, underneath each boob, was a tiny zip that could be opened to reveal the nipple. The baby got to feed, and the mother wasn't exposed at all. It was brilliant, and I loved Dominic that bit more for researching online and finding out about them when Bronagh expressed just how uncomfortable she felt when feeding in public.

Georgie *hated* being under a cover, and Bronagh *hated* not being able to use one, but now, it was all taken care of.

I couldn't wait to get some pieces of the clothing for my own wardrobe.

"Ow!" Bronagh suddenly hissed gaining both my and Dominic's attention.

I winced. "Did she bite you?"

Bronagh nodded as she adjusted her nipple in Georgie's mouth.

"One tiny tooth has cut through on her upper gum, and it's been grazin' me through nearly every feed."

"She'll learn to keep them away when her teeth cut through fully. Right now, it's probably irritatin' 'er too."

Bronagh nodded as she looked from Georgie to me. "She had us up for a few hours last night cryin'. 'Er cheeks were roarin' red, and she was gnawin' on everythin'. I put some teethin' rings in the freezer yesterday, and when I gave 'er one along with some teethin' gel to numb 'er gums, it relaxed 'er. The coolness and somethin' to chew on settled 'er and eventually put 'er back to sleep."

I frowned. "Teethin' sucks."

"I just hate that she's hurting, and we can't do much about it," Dominic said and leaned down to kiss Georgie's head.

Bronagh smiled at him then at me, she said, "You should have seen 'im. He was jumpin' around and pretendin' to get scared every time she screeched, which made 'er laugh. He was even singin' in an attempt to distract 'er from 'er pain. It was *so* cute."

I aww'd out loud, and Dominic glared at me then at Bronagh.

"I'm ripped with manliness," he said to her, puffing out his chest. "Don't call me cute."

Stupid thing to say.

"But you're me cutie mac cutie cute pie," my sister crooned.

I laughed while Dominic growled.

I looked down at my niece when she suddenly started crying.

"Georgie, baby, please don't do this again." Bronagh sighed.

I frowned. "What's wrong?"

"The last two weeks, she will latch on then unlatch and make sounds like she is heavin'. I've had to kind of sway her into feedin' lately, but it's like she is fightin' me on it. I can't remember the last time she just drank 'er fill and didn't fuss."

Uh-oh.

"It's buggin' me," Bronagh continued. "She's missed more than a whole feed nearly every day. When she *does* nurse, it doesn't last long, and it's messin' with me supply. I had to pump extra last night, but I didn't get much in the end."

I bit my lip, and my sister saw it.

"What?" she asked.

I shook my head in response.

"Branna," she pressed.

"I could be wrong," I said hesitantly. "She's probably coming down with somethin', or it could be 'er teethin', but it sounds like she is... self-weanin'."

"No." My sister laughed. "She's only four months old."

I tilted my head. "So?"

"So babies don't self-wean until they're *a lot* older."

I furrowed my brows. "What eejit told you that? Babies can self-wean at any time; it's just more common when they're older. All babies are different, and they don't follow a schedule. Besides, if your supply is low, she's probably gettin' annoyed with sucklin' and not gettin' much milk."

My sister stared at me then gasped. "Oh, my God. Branna."

I reached out and placed my hands on her arm at the same time Dominic placed his hands on her shoulders.

"She might not be weanin'; it might just be her teeth comin' through that's knockin' 'er off 'er routine, but just in case it *is* happenin', take a deep breath because this is *totally* normal. While it's not what you expected, this happens to many mammies. You can try 'er on a bottle and see how she takes it if you like?"

"I don't have any powdered milk; I've only ever breastfed—"

"I'll go to the store and get a box of the formula," Dominic cut Bronagh off. "I'll be back before you know it."

I told Dominic which brand to get then he took off jogging out of the bedroom. Almost instantly, my sister burst into tears as she stared down at her daughter, who was still fussing and pushing away from her breast. Eventually, Georgie abandoned feeding and just leaned against Bronagh and began to chew on her fingers, not interested in Bronagh's breast at all.

"I'm a horrible mother," Bronagh cried, her eyes filled with despair. "I can't even feed me own baby!"

"Hey, hey," I said softly and leaned over, hugging my sister. "This isn't you. This is all Georgie. She's eatin' some solid food for you now, and that can put her off wantin' milk, too. We always knew she was goin' to be an independent little madam, right?"

"Yeah, but when she was older." My sister sniffled. "Not now."

I frowned as she continued.

"I know I complain about nursin', but I don't mean it. I just get so tired sometimes."

"Bronagh," I said softly. "Every breastfeedin' mother goes through this at some point."

"I know," she cried. "I just didn't want it to be now."

I said nothing more; I simply comforted my sister. Nothing I said or did would make her feel better. She would have to come to terms with it on her own, and she would, in time. An hour after we realised why Georgie was acting up, she drank half of her formula bottle that Dominic bought in the supermarket and ate more than half a small bowl of pureed carrots. She *loved* her solid food, and having a full tummy brightened her up. She began talking in her baby language.

Loudly.

Bronagh said it was the first time in two weeks that she drank her fill of milk, had solid food on top of it, and didn't fight her on it, nor did she heave like she did when she breastfed. I saw it in my sister's eyes the moment she fully realised that Georgie was, quite possibly, self-weaning, and I could see that it cut her in two.

"She's you all over," I said to Bronagh to take her mind off it. "A big mouth."

Dominic tittered while my sister smiled lightly.

"Who's me favourite girl in the *whole* world?" I asked Georgie, who was now lying on my bed with me hovering over her.

"If you don't say me," my sister cut in, "I'm goin' to be extremely hurt."

Georgie laughed up at me, clapped her hands together, and kicked her chubby legs, which made me smile wide. She was in much better form now that she was fed.

"Tell Mammy to go away," I crooned.

Bronagh grumbled to herself, and whatever she said made Dominic snicker.

"I know," I said to my niece when she began talking in her own little language and blowing spit bubbles. "Tell me *all* about it... no way, did she really say that... oh, my God... what did you do... no, you didn't!"

The more I spoke to Georgie, the louder and more excited she became.

"What is my *wife* doing?"

My body went on high alert upon hearing his voice. My skin became hypersensitive, my breath caught, my nipples hardened, and yes, my clit pulsed to life. My reaction was that of a teenage boy who first discovered his right hand. I could only put *half* of it down to my new pregnancy hormones because the other half was purely my being a red-blooded woman turned on by everything about Ryder Slater.

I couldn't be blamed for it because my husband was *hot*.

"She's in a *very* intense discussion with Georgie," Dominic answered his brother. "You know... girl talk."

Ryder's chuckle sent a shiver up my spine.

"I'm not familiar with girl talk; I try to avoid it at all costs."

I snorted. "Please, we girl talk all the time. You just don't realise it's girl talk."

Dominic laughed at his brother but shut up when Bronagh said, "I don't know why you're laughin'. We girl talk all the time, *and* we watch *Teen Mom* together."

That was kind of Alec's fault. He got Kane and Dominic hooked on it after he realised one of the stars of the show was now a porn star of some kind. Of course, they all watched the porn video before the show itself, and now they just judge everyone and their parenting skills on the show. Only one of them was a father, but they all talked shit anyway.

"Quiet, woman," Dominic grumbled to my sister.

I snaked my hands under Georgie's armpits then lifted her up against my chest. I loved that she was much sturdier now. She was over four months old and was well and truly out of the newborn phase. She was awake more than she was asleep, she was loud—*so* bloody loud—and she liked her tummy time and watching cartoons on the television. All of that was only when I was babysitting her, though, so I could only imagine what she was like when she was at home with her parents. Everything about her would surely amplify.

"I'm gonna miss you," I said and gave her kisses all over her face, making her scream with laughter as she tried to 'eat' my face when it neared her mouth.

I knew Ryder was at my back before I turned around—I *felt* how close he was to me.

"Bee, quick," he began, "take the child before my wife changes her mind and bails on our honeymoon."

"Maybe I should leave Georgie with 'er, if that's the case."

Ryder growled at my sister while I chuckled.

"I'm fine," I assured him when I straightened up and turned around. "I'm just not lookin' forward to not seein' this puddin' for two weeks."

Ryder's expression softened, and he switched his gaze from me to our niece. He lifted his arms, held his hands out to Georgie, and she almost instantly leaned in his direction. She didn't raise her hands to go to anyone yet, but I had a feeling that would change over the coming weeks. The child had all of her uncles under her thumb, just as Jax did. All of the Slater brothers were big, bad, and took no bullshit... but if you put a baby in front of them, they became the biggest suckers known to man.

"I'm going to miss her too," Ryder said and kissed her chubby cheek.

Georgie rested her head on his shoulder as she used her hand to play with the ring on his necklace.

It was his wedding ring. He had to put it on a chain because he lost the bloody thing more times than I could count since we got married just three weeks ago. He wasn't used to wearing anything on his fingers, so when he took it off to wash his hands, he would sometimes forget to put it back on. Usually, it was in our bathroom or in our kitchen, but recently, he took it off in a public restroom to wash his hands and walked out without putting it back on. Luckily, he realised the second he left the restroom and ran back for it. That very day, he bought a long necklace and put the ring on it. He said he preferred it on the necklace because it was closer to his heart.

He was a charmer if I'd ever met one.

"Georgie," I said, gaining my niece's attention. "I love you."

She smiled at me, and it made us laugh because her bare gums showed... or her *almost* bare gums.

"I can see the tooth you mentioned, Bee," I said as I lifted my hand and placed my pinkie finger in Georgie's mouth so I could feel it.

"Branna, don't!"

"Ow!" I cried and snatched my hand away. "She *bit* me!"

Georgie laughed and so did Ryder and Dominic.

"I tried to warn you," my sister winced. "She bites *everythin'* now. Every. Thing."

I rubbed my thumb over my throbbing finger.

"That's the last time I put me fingers near *your* mouth," I said to Georgie and playfully narrowed my eyes.

"She'll learn not to put her fingers near *your* mouth either," Dominic mused.

I looked at him. "Why not?"

"Your surname is now Slater, but you're a Murphy at heart, and Murphy girls *bite*."

"That's true." Bronagh chirped. "Georgie is a Slater, but she's a Murphy, too. She'll be every bit like us."

"Heaven help me," Dominic said teasingly.

I snickered. "Oh, give over. We're harmless."

"When you're sleeping," Ryder commented.

I gasped. "How dare you!"

"My mistake." My husband smirked. "You still have some bite in you even when you sleep. I've the marks to prove it."

"It's your own fault for wakin' me up for sex; you *know* that never ends well for you."

"Bullshit." Ryder laughed. "Nine times out of ten, I get what I wake you up for."

I cocked a brow. "But there's still a chance it can go *very* wrong."

"It's worth the risk."

I tried not to smile but epically failed.

"You're both so cute that it's actually makin' me feel sick."

I looked at my sister. "Maybe you're just pregnant again."

Bronagh hissed. "Don't jinx me!"

"What's wrong with you being pregnant again?" Dominic asked, his tone displeased at his fiancée's obvious hiss of anger.

"Georgie is only four months old," my sister said in *duh* tone.

"So? Jax is ten months old, and Aideen isn't far off her due date with her second baby," Dominic countered.

"Aideen is a machine," Bronagh deadpanned. "I'm not."

"I want another baby, though," he said, no trace of humour in his tone.

I shared a look with Ryder who shook his head at me, silently telling me not to get involved. I mentally grunted because I was still learning to keep my nose out of my sister's relationship especially when an argument occurred in my presence.

"You can't make a baby *here*," I said, hoping to break the tension. "We're still present."

Dominic's lips twitched, indicating he'd heard me, but he didn't look away from Bronagh as he awaited her response. She was gnawing on her lower lip, her nervousness showing.

"But I've only got *six* pounds to go to get back to me pre-pregnancy weight."

If I heard about her weight or her diet one more time, I was going to kick her. It was all she talked about, and if it was grinding my gears, I could only imagine how much it peeved Dominic.

"Babe, *come on*. You had Georgie four months ago, and you already have the body of wet dreams," he said and pulled her against his chest. "You know I want five kids, at least, and *you* were the one who said you wanted them to be close in age."

Bronagh narrowed her eyes. "Don't use me own words against me, Fuckface."

I playfully gasped as I reached over and covered Georgie's ears. "Language!"

Dominic grinned at Bronagh when she cringed as she looked at me and said, "Sorry."

I looked down at my niece when I removed my hands and said, "Your Mammy has a sailor's mouth."

"Ain't that the truth," Dominic said then grunted when I guessed Bronagh socked him one in the stomach.

"Four more," he rasped. "That was the deal."

"You made a deal on how many kids you were both havin'?" I asked on a snicker.

"We talked about it midway through me pregnancy with Georgie," Bronagh said with a grunt. "Dominic and the brothers have this weird thing about the number five. There are five of them, so they each want five kids."

I remembered Keela calling Alec and asking him about that a couple of years ago, and he mentioned the same thing, but I thought it was just a joke.

"Well, *I'm* not havin' five kids," I firmly stated. "I'm thirty-three and don't plan on spendin' the rest of me thirties pregnant."

My sister instantly looked at Ryder.

"You've gone and done it now," she said then grinned at me when I glared at her.

"Why not, Bran?" Ryder asked me, stepping between me and my sister to force my focus on him.

I shrugged. "'Cause it's a lot of kids."

"Yeah," Ryder agreed. "It is, but it's a good number."

For him maybe.

"We're both thirty-three, if I have four more after this one, it'll take *years* to pop them all out. That's not addin' in the time it would take to *get* pregnant. We got lucky on this baby, but it doesn't always work out like that. Sometimes tryin' can take a *long* time."

Especially the older you get.

"Branna, we *aren't* old," Ryder said with a shake of his head. "We're in our early thirties. Since when is that old?"

"Since I started havin' to dye me hair every *three feckin' months* to hide me grey hairs!"

I still felt sick about that. My roots weren't growing out as dark brown anymore; they were growing out a lighter brown and *grey*. I was only thirty-three, and my pigment was fading. It broke my damn heart.

"Mate, really?" Bronagh winced from behind Ryder. "That *sucks*."

I threw my hands up in the air.

"See!" I stated. "Bronagh knows the importance of hair and what goin' grey means."

It meant I was getting old.

"People can get grey hairs from anything, not just growing old,"

Dominic commented. "I'd put it down to stress in your case. You've been through a hell of a lot over the last year and a half, *and* you have a hectic job."

I leaned to my right and narrowed my eyes.

"Butt out, Slater."

He clamped his mouth shut, but the corners of his lips turned up in a grin. I looked back at Ryder then quickly down at Georgie when she started to sing a song of sorts.

I beamed at her. "You have a *lovely* singin' voice, me love."

"We're *not* done with this conversation," Ryder said, amused that I was point-blank ignoring him. "We have two whole weeks to straighten this out, and you can't hide from me where we're going."

My heart jumped.

"Promises, promises," I teased.

Ryder growled, and it made me grin.

Oh, yeah, this was going to be a *fun* honeymoon.

CHAPTER TWO

"**B**ad news, Sweetness."

My heart stopped at Ryder's words. A terrifying flash-back of being in my kitchen many years ago and him telling me Bronagh had been abducted played in my mind, and a sick feeling of dread swirled in my abdomen.

"What is it?" I nervously asked as I gripped the handle of my suitcase.

I was in the middle of wheeling it out to the hallway to leave it next to the front door of our house.

"We can't leave until tomorrow." He frowned, his shoulders sagging. "Heavy rain is due this evening, and I don't want to take the risk with you in the car."

My physical reaction mirrored Ryder's. My shoulders slumped in disappointment, and my face fell, but my heart practically deflated with relief. I was gutted that we had to wait one more day for our getaway, but bad news from one of the brothers usually meant one of them telling me my sister or one of my friends were in serious danger, so this piece of news was easier to digest, but I couldn't tell Ryder that.

"It's fine," I assured him when he frowned deeper at my reaction. "It's only one night, right?"

He quickly nodded. "The storm breaks during the night, so we can leave in the a.m."

I looked down at my big suitcase next to Ryder's small duffle bag and said, "Well, at least we're already packed."

I looked back at my husband and smiled up at him when he stepped forward and pressed his body against mine. My pulse spiked when his hands went straight to my behind. I startled when Ryder captured my lips in a surprise kiss. I lifted my arms and placed my hands on his shoulders, digging my nails into his skin. He hissed, and it gave me the opportunity to snag his lower lip with my teeth. I gently bit down then sucked on it. I hummed when I felt his body shudder.

"Need you," he rasped.

He *needed* me.

I released his lip. "You've got me, honey."

Ryder backed me up against the wall in the hallway, and it made me giggle.

"In the hall?" I asked then groaned when his lips went to my neck, and he zeroed in on my sweet spot. "But Damien—"

"Is over at Dominic's," my husband cut me off, his breathing laboured.

Where Dominic was, Damien wasn't far away.

I hummed. "You dirty man."

I heard Ryder's zipper being lowered, and I felt his rushed movements as he pushed down his jeans, quickly following suit with my leggings and underwear as he shoved them down to my knees. He carefully turned me until my back pressed against his front. His excitement and obvious hunger for me caused heat to spread between my thighs almost instantly.

"You've got me fumbling like a prepubescent boy," he growled, and slapped my bare arse.

I looked over my shoulder and grinned. "You're *all* man, baby."

"You bet your sweet ass I am."

He disappeared as he dropped to his knees behind me, and that movement was the only indication I got to what he was doing a second before I felt his tongue plunge into my exposed cunt.

"Oh, *fuck*!"

I gripped onto the side table closest to me and forced my knees not to buckle. My excitement quickly changed to an urgent need. My clit throbbed, each pulse acting as a demand for the attention of Ryder's skilled tongue. I let go of the table with my right hand with the intention of stroking my clit myself, but a sharp wave of desire struck my body, and I needed to hold the table to stay upright.

Sex for me during this pregnancy had so far proved to be *awesome*. Every lick, stroke, thrust, and bump felt unbelievably amazing. I was so sensitive that the littlest of touches got me off. Coming early, and often, was *not* something that embarrassed me. I embraced the hell out of it and so did my husband.

"So sensitive," Ryder growled against my sensitive flesh as he plunged his tongue deep into me once more.

"Ryder," I moaned, trying not to buck back against his face. "Me clit, please."

He nudged my knees apart with his hand, which was hard to do since my leggings were bundled around my shins, but he used the space and placed his hands on my legs and slowly moved upwards, massaging my inner thighs along the way. I held my breath when his thumb dipped into my pussy then slid over my lips as he neared my aching clit. The first touch sent a spasm throughout my body, and I knew I was a few seconds away from release. Ryder did too.

He bore down and rotated his thumb in a delicious circle that, quite literally, took my breath away. For a second or two, time itself stopped, and a feeling close to pain flared before sheer bliss replaced it. Pulse after pulse of ecstasy washed over me in waves, and if it wasn't for Ryder's hold on me, I would have dropped to the ground like a sack of potatoes. When the throbbing of delight slowed and eventually subsided, I opened my eyes, and instead of saying something sassy to my husband, a strangled cry of delight left my mouth as Ryder drove his length into the depths of my body.

"Heaven," he growled. "You feel like Heaven. Every." *Thrust.*

"Single." *Thrust.* "Time." *Thrust.*

I re-established my hold on the table before me and held on for dear life. Ryder's fingers bit into my flesh when his hold on my hips tightened. I didn't need to ask if he was okay because the quickened paced of his thrusting told me just how good he was.

"Fuck, Sweetness," he moaned. "Not gonna last long today, you feel too perfect."

I hummed in response and pushed back against him, meeting him thrust for thrust.

"Like a fucking vice," he hissed.

Ryder slammed into me once, twice, thrice, and then his motions became jerked as he came.

"*Branna*," he roared.

I leaned forward, pressing my cheek against the cool wooden surface of the table, and tried to catch my breath. It was only at that moment that I realised just how breathless I was, and I was worried that I sounded like someone who had just ran a marathon.

"Baby?" Ryder said, placing a hand on my back. "Are you okay?"

"Fine," I rasped.

He withdrew from me, and I frowned at the loss. I *loved* sex with Ryder; the connection of him being inside me was like nothing I had ever felt before.

"You don't sound okay," he said as he straightened me up and nudged me backwards so he could move in front of me and look down at me. I inhaled and exhaled twice before I replied.

"You're goin' to kill me one day," I joked. "Killer sex. That'd be a good way to go."

Ryder frowned. "Don't joke about that."

My lips twitched. "Sorry."

He brushed my hair out of my face and simply stared down at me.

I blushed. "What?"

"Your breathing," he said, his tone firm. "It's been getting

21

worse. Any sort of activity tires you out almost instantly, and you struggle for your breath."

His attentiveness was going to give him a panic attack one day.

"I *am* pregnant, Ry. Breathlessness is normal, and the bigger I get, the more breathless I will become. I'll be able to tell if it becomes a problem, though, okay? Don't worry so much."

"You're my wife, and you're pregnant with our child. Worrying is all I've done these past three weeks."

I reached up and pressed my palm against his cheek.

"I'm okay. I promise."

He sighed. "Okay."

I winked then bent down to pull my underwear and leggings up, but Ryder beat me to it. When I was decent, I went upstairs to the bathroom to clean myself up. When I exited the bathroom, Ryder was leaning against the wall facing me, and I couldn't help but laugh at him.

"Did you think I was goin' to fall down the toilet?"

He snorted. "You'd make anything possible, Sweetness."

I crossed the landing to him. He leaned his head down and rubbed the tip of his nose over my cheek when I came to a stop before him. I smiled wider when I felt his hands touch my stomach.

"I feel like there's something between us," he joked as he ran his hands over my growing baby bump.

My lips curved upward. "Just your *active* child."

I felt the baby kick at that moment. It was if he or she knew they were the topic of conversation. Ryder smiled when a second thump came from my womb. He ran this thumb over the exact spot and said, "I can't wait until you're big enough that I can *see* the baby move in your belly."

I cringed. "I *can* wait because that has always and *will* always freak me out."

Ryder chuckled and kissed my forehead. "I love you."

He told me that at least ten times a day since we made up a few months ago. He said he was making up for all the days he didn't tell me when we hit our rough patch, making sure that every day forward I knew just how deep his love ran for me.

"I love you, too," I replied, meaning the words with every fibre of my being.

He gave me a squeeze then said, "Dominic is worried about Bronagh."

Sickness churned in my gut.

"I know." I swallowed. "She will be a little depressed for a while if Georgie is truly weanin'. She tried to smile and act like she didn't feel so deeply about it, but I could see how close she was to breakin' down when they were leavin' earlier."

"Dominic called while you were in the restroom and said he brought Georgie to Gravity with him and Damien just to give Bee some time to herself. He said she keeps crying when she looks at the baby."

My heart hurt.

"I'm goin' to go over there and spend a couple of hours with 'er just so she's not alone. I have the time since we're here for another night. I don't know how she feels, but I know it's not somethin' she should deal with alone. She'll send Dominic away so she doesn't worry 'im but not me."

"I'll drive you."

I gave Ryder a stern look. "I'll drive meself since I'm not big enough *yet* to need assistance."

Thank God.

My husband's lips thinned to a line, showcasing his disappointment.

I place my hands on my already expanding hips. "Say whatever it is you want to say."

He didn't hesitate.

"I don't feel comfortable with you—"

"Drivin'?" I finished. "I don't understand *why*."

"You're pregnant, Branna."

Very perceptive of you.

"I'm aware of that, honey, but it doesn't mean I can't drive. I'm not goin' to stress and worry about everythin' that *could* happen durin' this pregnancy, okay? I refuse to live me life in fear."

I lived like that once, and I vowed never to spend another minute lost in the darkness of that kind of dread.

Ryder still wasn't happy that I clung to my independence so quickly after the horrid things I had endured a few months ago. I think he preferred when I didn't want to go out by myself, but luckily, he relented and nodded once, accepting my decision. I leaned up on my tiptoes and pecked his lips to show my appreciation for him dropping the matter even though I knew it was hard for him to lighten up on the 'Branna protection detail'.

"I'll call you as soon as I get there if it makes you feel any better?"

He gripped my waist tightly with his large hands.

"It would."

I winked. "Consider it done."

"We can talk about future babies when you get back," he said nonchalantly.

I rubbed the base of my neck. "Ry—"

"Later."

He kissed my forehead, turned, and headed downstairs and into the kitchen, leaving me to stare after him. When he was out of my sight, I shook my head at his pig-headedness and headed downstairs then out of the house. Twenty minutes later, I was parking Ryder's car—no, *our* car—in the driveway of Dominic and Bronagh's house. It was vacant since Dominic wasn't there. I unbuckled my seatbelt and got out of the car. I used my house key to let myself in. I had promised to respect Bronagh's family privacy and swore to only use my key for emergencies, but this *was* kind of an emergency, so I was putting it to good use.

"Bee?" I called out as I closed the door behind me.

When silence answered me, I frowned.

"Bronagh?" I shouted louder.

I checked the sitting room and kitchen, and when I found they were empty, I headed upstairs, but there was no sign of her or anyone in any of the rooms.

"Where the hell are you?" I mumbled to myself as I dug out my phone from my pocket and dialled my sister's number.

"'Ello?" a voice that wasn't my sister's answered on the fourth ring.

"Keela?" I said, confused. "Why do you have Bronagh's phone?"

"It's a *long* feckin' story, Bran," she grumbled. "I tried ringin' you, but the reception block in this area is shite. Where are you?"

"I'm in Bronagh's house," I answered, placing my free hand on my hip. "Ryder told me Dominic went out with Georgie and Damien to Gravity so she could have some time to 'erself. We're pretty sure Georgie is self-weanin' from breastfeedin', and Bronagh's havin' a rough time with it."

"Oh, I heard *all* about it."

"So she's with you then?" I asked. "I thought maybe she came by to see you and forgot 'er phone at your place and that's how you have it."

"Nope, I'm with 'er. Alannah too."

Why does she sound so weird?

"What's the problem?" I questioned.

"Ask me where I am," Keela said in a huffed breath.

I blinked. "Okay, where are you?"

"In Crough's Pub."

"Fuck."

"Yeah, everythin' about this is *fuck*."

Bollocks.

"So," Keela continued.

I groaned. "*So?*"

"Alannah and Bronagh," she began.

"What about them?"

"They're... well... they're... drunk."

"Oh, Jesus," I paled. "Not again."

"Yep, *again.*"

The gates of Hell have reopened.

I closed my eyes. "Are you sure?"

"Oh, I'm sure." Keela snorted. "Alannah is twerkin', and Bronagh is strippin' off. You might wanna call the lads 'cause they won't listen to me—ah fuck, they're gettin' up to sing karaoke. I need backup!"

"I'll be there ASAP."

I hung up on Keela, dialled Dominic's number, and was glad when he answered on the third ring.

"Houston." I sighed. "We have a big arse problem."

CHAPTER THREE

"**A**m I supposed to know what that means?" Dominic questioned.

Yes.

"What're you doin'?"

"I'm at Gravity with Damien and Georgie. They added an infant and toddler section with these cute as fuck walls that are no taller than I am. We put a harness on her and let her 'climb' it. She screamed and laughed the entire time. We got it on video—wait till you see it, it's fucking adorable."

"Yeah, I can't wait to see it... so listen, I've somethin' to tell you."

Things got quiet on Dominic's end.

"What's wrong?" he asked.

"Bronagh and Alannah." I exhaled as I looked up at the ceiling. "They're causin' Keela problems."

"How?" he quizzed. "Are they still telling her they won't pose for a nude photo shoot to be on the cover of her book?"

My lips twitched. "She was messin' with them about that."

"Then what're they doing?" he asked before quickly saying, "Ah-ah, baby. No. Daddy is talking on the phone; you can't play with it. No. Ah-ah. Georgie. No hitting, baby. I said *no!*"

A loud cry came from the receiver of my phone, and it caused

27

me to wince.

"Damien!" Dominic called. "Take her for a second; I can't hear what Branna is saying over her fussing."

I heard Damien's voice as he cooed and spoke to Georgie in a soft tone; both his voice and my niece's shouting faded away, and I heard Dominic's deep sigh.

"This breast weaning thing is giving me a headache, and it's on-ly starting."

I laughed. "Imagine how Bronagh feels."

"Speaking of my future wife, what has she and Alannah done to grind Keela's gears?"

Here we go.

"Do you want it straight or watered down?"

"Like you even have to ask." He snorted. "Straight all day every day, baby."

You asked for it.

"They're both drunk in Crough's pub," I blurted. "Keela can on-ly do so much to contain them when they're together like this. Kara-oke is involved and alcohol is involved, which means—"

"Horrible dancing and stripping are involved," Dominic fin-ished.

"Pretty much."

"I'll be there in fifteen minutes," he angrily stated then shouted, "Dame, you aren't goin' to *believe* this shit. Get the baby ready. We're leaving. *Now.*"

I pulled my phone away from my ear and looked at the screen when silence dragged on, indicating Dominic hung up. He sounded pissed, and I didn't blame him. Drunk Bronagh, was... crazy. Crazier than sober Bronagh, which was saying something.

With a shake of my head, I left my sister's house and got into my car. I backed out of the garden and headed in the direction of Crough's pub. I needed to get there before Dominic and Damien did to act as a barricade to protect Bronagh. Dominic would never hurt her, but he'd give her a right talking to, and even *that* could be too intense for public.

Ten minutes later, as I pulled up to the pub and parked, my phone rang. I fumbled with my bag to grab my device, and when I saw it was my husband calling me, I winced, realising I forgot to call him to let him know I was okay.

"Hey," I said in a rushed breath when I answered. "Sorry, I didn't ring. I've a—"

"Big ass problem," Ryder said, cutting me off. "I heard all 'bout it. Dominic just dropped Georgie off with me and told me where he and Dame were heading and why. Just giving you a heads-up that he's pissed. Really pissed. Damien isn't faring better either. You know how he gets when it comes to Alannah."

Shite.

"Brilliant," I grumbled as I climbed out of the car and locked it up. "I'll be home when I square everythin' away 'ere."

"Good luck." Ryder laughed.

I hung up on him, shook my head, and entered the pub. It wasn't hard to find my sister and friend. In fact, it was quite possibly the easiest task ever bestowed upon me. On a cramped stage in the corner of the pub, both girls jammed out to some God-awful music with no lyrics, just horribly loud siren sounds.

I spotted Keela sitting at the bar, watching the girls with a shake of her head. I moved towards her and took up the vacant stool next to her, gaining her attention. She leaned over and gave me a hug in greeting.

"The barman told me they've only been 'ere about forty minutes," she said as she retook her seat. "They're both buckled, though."

"Bee hasn't drank in forever with bein' pregnant and breast feedin'," I commented, "and Lana hardly ever lets loose... They're the perfect lightweights."

Keela snorted. "You're tellin' me."

"Bee must be sure that Georgie is weanin' in order to be drinkin' alcohol. Lana is drunk probably because she is dealin' with the knowledge of her da's secret affair *and* with Damien bein' home—even though she won't admit she feels any sort of way about his return."

"That's exactly what I'm thinkin'. *They* think they're havin' fun, but deep down, they know better. Right now, drinkin' is a vice."

"This might end in tears." I sighed.

"Or laughter," Keela mused. "I get why they're drinkin', but when they drink, it's pretty funny for everyone in close proximity to them."

I thought back to the last time they got drunk together, and my lips curved upwards.

"I guess we'll find out."

I turned and ordered an ice water when familiar music began to play, and familiar voices began to sing.

Oh, God.

I looked at Keela, who faced the bar like me. We turned back around, but Keela kept her eyes closed, and it made me laugh.

"Are they... *singin'* karaoke?" she asked. "Really singin' it? Not just mumblin' along?"

I nodded as she opened her eyes and winced as both my sister and friend drunkenly jammed out on the small stage in the corner of the pub. Even though the place was small, the two of them still drew an audience.

"Me milkshake brings all the boys to the yard, and they're like; it's better than yours—"

"This is bad," Keela said, then covered her mouth when Alannah began to twerk.

I widened my eyes. "Why does she turn into Beyoncé when she is drunk but is quiet as a mouse when sober?"

"Maybe this is the real Lana, and we've only known a cover-up version of 'er?"

I shook my head. "I'm inclined to believe you because... *damn.* She used to suck but has clearly been practicin'. I mean how does she make 'er arse move like that?"

"Don't look at me; I can't twerk to save me life," Keela replied. "The only thing that shakes on me is me belly rolls."

"Same 'ere, babe." I laughed. "Same 'ere."

Bronagh and Alannah messed up on the song lyrics of *Milkshake* by Kelis, which grabbed our attention. My sister then sighed through the microphone. Looking down at her chest, she said to Alannah, "Me boobs are useless and ha-have no purpose an-anymore."

Their voices carried, earning them hoots and cheers.

Alannah laughed. "Your baby daddy wo-would disagree."

Bronagh looked at her then they both laughed and cried, which only made me shake my head.

"They're a sorry mess."

"I think they're both hilarious." Keela chuckled. "We never get to see them like this."

Both of the girls ended up on the floor of the stage seconds after they began to laugh, and it gave me a slight headache just wondering how I'd get them into my car.

"We need more backup," I admitted. "I don't think we can handle them ourselves, and Dame and Dominic are takin' their sweet time."

Keela winced. "You wanna call Kane and Alec?"

I nodded. "Aideen has Jax, and she is too far along in 'er pregnancy to be of any real help. Ryder has Georgie, so he can't help."

Keela gnawed on her lower lip then quickly said, "Bagsy not callin' them."

"Mother of fuck!" I groaned.

I took out my phone and dialled Kane's number.

"Hi, Branna," he said on the third ring.

"Hey, Kane, are you busy?"

"I'm tidying up while Aideen and Jax nap."

Aw.

"You're adorable."

He grunted in response.

"*Super* adorable."

"Woman," he growled.

"Someone's grumpy."

"Sorry." Kane sighed. "It's just Aideen. I asked her to do something earlier, and she did the complete opposite of what I wanted and killed my boner."

"How dare she."

"Right?"

I shook my head, smiling.

"What'd she do?" I quizzed.

"I asked her to send me a picture of something that she thought would excite me, and do you know what she sent me?"

"No," I replied. "But I desperately want to know."

"She sent me a picture of a jar of Nutella."

I laughed. Hard.

"Hanging up now."

"No," I pleaded. "I'm so sorry. I'll stop. It's really not that funny."

It's fucking hilarious.

"What do you want, Bran?" He sighed.

"Nothing since you're *clearly* busy."

"Dante is here to watch Aideen if you need help with something?"

"Well," I said and stretched the L. "Me and Keela could really use your and Alec's help right about now. Bronagh and Alannah are mindlessly drunk, and I've *no* idea where Dominic and Damien are to help us with gettin' them home and—"

"We're here."

I screamed, and so did Keela. We both spun around to face Dominic and Damien who had silently walked up behind us. They both had hard stares on their identical faces, and looked meaner than Hell. I pressed my free hand to my chest while Dominic reached forward and plucked my phone from my hold.

"Bro?" he said, probably because he didn't know which brother

I was talking to. "No need to do anything; Dame and I have this."

Kane spoke, and Dominic was silent as he listened.

"Yeah, they've been drinking in a pub, and the girls called us to get them home. No need to worry. Like I said, we've got this. Yeah... no problem. Okay. Bye."

He handed me back my phone then looked over my shoulder and shook his head.

"How much have they had to drink?" he asked, his eyes focused behind me.

Keela shrugged. "Not a lot, they're just lightweights."

The lads humourlessly snorted.

"Bee's kept her clothes on her this time," Damien mused, earning a vicious scowl from Dominic.

"She *was* strippin' earlier," Keela chimed in, not caring that the lads were pissed, "but the barman told 'er it wasn't the kind of establishment where she could do that without gettin' thrown out. Lana's gotten better at twerkin' too."

Damien grunted at Keela's comment while Dominic pinched the bridge of his nose.

"I shouldn't have left her." He sighed. "I should have stayed with her."

I nudged him. "Don't beat yourself up about it, kid. Bee didn't want you around, which is why she sent you off with Georgie to Gravity. She is beatin' 'erself up about Georgie weanin' so early, but she will realise it had nothin' to do with 'er, it's just that Georgie doesn't want to do it anymore."

"Yeah," he said, but looked at Bronagh with a longing of sorts.

I knew he wanted to take her pain away because it was exactly what I wanted, but I knew my job was to comfort her and simply be there for her. Dominic would realise his role until Bronagh came to grips with the new change in her everyday routine by herself.

"So," I said, looking to change the subject. "How are we goin' to do this?"

Instead of furthering our conversation, we all looked at one another when a familiar tune began to play.

"'Hot Stuff,'" Keela said with a laugh.

She was correct—Alannah and Bronagh were about to sing "Hot Stuff" by Donna Summer.

"If I have to deal with this, I might as well grab a front row seat," Dominic said, licking his lips.

He shared a look with his brother then, without warning, they shot forward, shoving other punters aside until they both got a seat directly in front of the stage Bronagh and Alannah were making their own.

"Do you think we should record this?" I asked Keela as the brothers made themselves at home.

I looked at her when she didn't reply and laughed when I saw she already had her phone out and pointed at the stage. Keela looked at me and grinned. "If they tell me to delete it tomorrow, I will, but they *have* to see the shite they do when they're drunk. They're nightmares."

I blessed myself. "Amen to that."

The girls began singing, not noticing Dominic and Damien in the audience, and they gave it their all, which meant they crowed like birds and shuffled around the stage. The only time they were in sync was when Donna Summer sang the words "Hot stuff". They both hip thrusted forward as if they were humping someone. It caused me to laugh so hard that I cried. Keela, who was in a heap laughing, turned the camera on me, but I waved her away when I had to cross my legs to avoid wetting myself.

"*Why* do they have to hip thrust?" I asked as tears of laughter fell from my eyes.

Keela couldn't reply; her laughter wouldn't allow it. I fanned myself with my hands to cool and calm myself down. I wiped under my eyes and shook my head at the two idiots on the stage, but silently thanked them for the entertainment. Towards the end of the song, things got a little raunchy. Bronagh swayed her hips from side to side as she sang, and Alannah... well, she just surprised the heck out of me.

"Omigod." I blinked. "Did Lana just slut drop?"

Keela bobbed her head up and down. "She did, and fuck me if she didn't nail it."

"This isn't fair," I complained. "They were shite dancers last year, and now all of a sudden, they've got moves. *Sexy* moves. I don't understand."

"They're fast learners, it appears." Keela snorted.

When the song ended, I said, "Thank God for that. They're so funny, but they can't sing for shite."

Keela chuckled as she bumped fists with me in agreement.

"How long do you think it'll take before they realise we're 'ere?" Keela asked.

"About—"

"Dominic!" Bronagh's squeal cut me off. "Girls! You came!"

"A whole second," I finished, chuckling.

My sister stumbled off the stage, and if it wasn't for Dominic's quick reaction catching her, she'd have fallen on her face.

"Another drink." She laughed when he lugged her over to the bar.

"You've had *more* than enough, Bronagh," Dominic protested, keeping his hands on her. "You're coming home."

My sister glared up at him. "You can't te-tell me wh-what to do."

"Watch me," Dominic countered, and levelled her with a glare of his own.

Bronagh, as usual, didn't back down and neither did Dominic— surprise, surprise.

I chimed in and said, "Bronagh, you both need to go home so you can get Georgie fed and put down for the night."

My sister's eyes filled with tears. "I can't feed 'er, Branna."

"Sis." I frowned and stepped forward, gathering her in my arms. "It's goin' to be okay, I promise. There is *nothin'* wrong with you or Georgie; she is just ready to move on from breastfeedin'. I know you aren't ready for this change, but she is, so we've all got to roll with the punches."

Bronagh nodded against my shoulder but said nothing; she only cried. I looked up at Dominic, whose eyes were on my sister. He hurt for her, and it was then that I knew she would be okay. Bronagh and Georgie were his life, and he'd give everything up if it meant their happiness. I knew he would take care of her when I couldn't.

"It's time to go home with Dominic," I said, smiling as I pulled back from our hug. "You will get through this together as a family, okay?"

She nodded, but I could see she still wasn't convinced. And that was okay because the acceptance wouldn't happen overnight.

"I wanna sing again!" Alannah suddenly announced as Keela helped keep her upright.

"Singing?" Damien grinned, making sure to stay out of her view. "Is *that* what you call it?"

Alannah slid her eyes to his, and they widened almost instantly.

"Snowflake!" she squealed. "You made it!"

She stumbled away from Keela and over to Damien who was *more* than willing to hold her up.

"I came," he said, chuckling. "How are you?"

"You're here, so I'm gr-great," she replied and leaned her head against his chest.

Damien looked at me and Keela, his brother, and then back down at Alannah.

"What do you say I bring you home?" he suggested.

"I say," she paused to hiccup then continued, "that's a br-brilliant idea."

Bronagh looked at Alannah and laughed. "You can't ha-have sex with 'im."

Alannah pulled a face at her. "I ca-can if I want to!"

Damien widened his eyes then glanced around and said, "I'd never touch her. Not when she's like this. I swear."

Dominic snorted. "You don't have to assure us. We know it'd

be Lana trying it on with you. She's drunk; it's the only time she has any courage."

"Shut up, Dominic," Damien grumbled.

Alannah, who was standing right next to Dominic when he spoke, yawned like she didn't hear a word that was just spoken. She leaned her head back and looked up at Damien.

"Who is your favourite fictional ch-character?" she slurred.

Damien furrowed his brows. "Uh, I guess it's Bugs Bunny?"

"Want to know mine?" she asked, her voice turning sultry.

Damien nodded, licking his lower lip.

"Mine is Jack Frost."

I wonder why.

Damien held Alannah tightly. "Nice choice."

She gave him a thumbs-up before quickly saluting him.

I raised my brows. "Lana, what the heck are you doin'?"

"Damien and Dominic," she said like whatever she was thinking was obvious.

I blinked. "What about them?"

"They're the pilots in the cockpit!" she announced as she extended her arms and began to 'fly' around us whilst making aeroplane noises.

Bronagh was completely unfazed as her twenty-three-year-old friend zoomed around us pretending to be an aeroplane. My sister locked eyes on her man and said, "I'll jump in *your* cockpit, Captain Slater."

"My *God*, woman!" Dominic hissed, sucking a deep breath through his teeth.

"Do you have a boardin' pass?" Alannah asked Damien, pausing during her 'flight' long enough to speak. "You can't enter the cockpit without a boardin' pass. Airline rules."

"Yeah," Damien answered, and I saw how hard he was trying to hold his laughter in. "What airline is that, good looking?"

"Bad Bitches Airways," Alannah said without missing a beat.

I shared a look with Dominic, Damien, and Keela, and at the exact same time, we all burst into laughter.

"What so fu-funny, fuckers?" she then asked, before stumbling into Damien who grabbed her.

"Okay, Freckles, time to go." He smiled, and it made me smile, too. I only saw him smile like this around Alannah, and the kid was oblivious to it.

"You're *my* Jack Frost. You know that, right?" Alannah said as she leaned into Damien and lifted her hand to his white-blond hair. "Mine."

Damien closed his eyes. "You're breaking my heart here, Freckles."

"You broke mine a long time ago."

I saw Damien's shoulders slump, and my heart hurt for him.

"I know," he said, reopening his eyes, "but I'm trying real hard to make up for it."

Alannah bobbed her head up and down. "I know."

"You do?" he asked, surprised.

"I do," she said.

"Well, okay then."

I looked at Keela when both he and Alannah began to 'walk' out of the pub. Both of them laughed at Alannah's stumbling with each step she took.

"What just happened?" I asked her.

"I think," she began, "Alannah just acknowledged that Damien has been tryin' to make up for what he did to 'er... but she's hammered, so maybe it doesn't count."

I folded my arms across my chest.

"You could be right, *or* it could be that a drunken mind is speakin' a sober heart."

"We've all have our problems with the lads." Keela sighed. "I've had me fair share with Alec. God knows I've dealt with things I thought I'd never have to... but Lana's situation is different. Damien has been in 'er head and heart since she was a kid. What went down between them... that's a lot of pain to be carryin' around with you for five years. Watchin' your friends bein' loved up with his brothers has to be hard, and to see 'er *best* friend in a steady relationship with his *twin*? Man, that's *got* to be hell. We don't even know their *real* feelins'; we only know what's been shared. It runs deeper than just a one-night stand that happened years ago. It has to."

I linked arms with my friend.

"Whatever the outcome with the pair of them, we'll help them through it," I said firmly. "It's what family is for."

Always.

"Stop being a ca-caveman," my sister's voice warned from behind us, causing both Keela and me to turn around. "Just because you're the one with the di-dick here doesn't make you th-the boss." She pointed her chest. "*I'm* the boss. Me."

Dominic looked at us then back at his lady. "We all know you're the boss, but that doesn't mean I won't redden your ass if you don't get it in gear and move."

Bronagh narrowed her eyes, so Dominic stepped forward.

"Test me on this," he said, his voice gruff. "I dare you."

She lost her nerve and backed down.

"Okay, bossy arse," she mumbled.

Dominic's lips twitched. "I'm still going to redden your ass."

Bronagh widened her eyes. "I th-thought you were playin'!"

"I *never* play when it comes to your ass," Dominic said, smirking.

"Unfair!" My sister groaned.

I hid my grin as the pair of batshit crazies walked out of the pub hand in hand. Granted, the handholding this time around was mainly because Bronagh could barely walk unassisted. Either way, it was still cute. Keela and I followed them, and once we saw the lads had the girls' safely into Dominic and Bronagh's car, we both got into my car and drove home.

"How'd you get 'ere if you don't have your car?" I asked Keela as I pulled onto the main road.

"I did this crazy thing... I walked."

I bit down on my lip. "Smartarse."

Keela snorted. "Alec has our car, so I didn't have a choice. Me Uncle Brandon rang and said one of his lads saw 'Rampage's misses' and 'er 'hot friend' drinkin' heavily in Crough's. I told 'im thanks for the heads up then headed down there to try and get them home without causin' problems, but we know how well *that* turned out."

I nodded. "They're funny as hell, but my God, they're a handful, especially when together."

"They'll be dyin' sick tomorrow."

I evilly grinned. "I'm countin' on it."

Keela laughed then we chatted back and forth until I arrived home. We passed Dominic's car as I neared my house, and a glance and a wave told me he'd collected Georgie from Ryder. When I pulled into my driveway, I leaned over and hugged Keela in farewell. She left and walked across the street to her and Alec's home.

The front door to my house was open, and Ryder filled the space. My heart skipped a beat as I took him in. Both of his arms raised above his head where he held onto the top of the door's panel. He was shirtless—obviously—and every muscle the man possessed was flexed, practically *begging* me to lick them in greeting.

"Branna?"

I looked up when I heard my name.

"Hmmm?"

Ryder's lips twitched. "I was talking to you, but you weren't listening."

"I was listenin'." I grinned. "Just not to you."

To my body.

His eyes flicked down, and he leisurely rolled his eyes over said body as I strode towards him.

"You're edible."

I hummed. "I bet I am."

His eyes flashed with amusement.

"You seem very upbeat, so I guess it went okay?"

"Epically brilliant doesn't cover it," I gleamed. "But Keela's video will. She's goin' to send it to me so I can show you."

Ryder laughed as he lowered his arms and encircled them around me as I came to a stop and leaned my body against his. I looked over my shoulder when I heard a whistle. I waved when I saw it was Alec from across the road. He had just pulled into his driveway and was getting out of his car. He locked his car and jogged over to us.

"Hey guys."

I hugged him in greeting while Ryder did the bro-hug thing they always did when they saw each other.

"Hey." I smiled. "You're home late."

"Picking up dinner," he said, and gestured to the bag that I noticed him carrying. "Keela called and said she had an interesting video to show me."

I laughed. "Why do you look so excited?"

"It might be porn!"

I face palmed. "That is *such* an Alec thing to say."

"Nah, it's a man thing." He winked. "We relate everything to sex, and if we say otherwise, we're lying."

"Thanks for that," Ryder mumbled as he rested his chin on my head, earning a grin from me.

I focused on Alec. "The video isn't porn."

"Excuse me?" he said, frowning. "How do you know?"

"Because I was there when the video—"

"You're *in* a porno?" Alec gasped. "For real?"

Ryder laughed. I scowled.

"No," I stated. "It's *not* a porno."

Alec's shoulders slumped. "Well, that just ruined my entire day."

I resisted the urge to laugh.

"I'm sorry to hear that."

He turned and began to walk away, mumbling something to himself.

"Bye," I called out.

"Yeah, yeah. Bye," he replied, and practically dragged his feet as he walked back to his house. I shook my head.

"I love 'im so much," I said to my husband while watching his brother walk home. "He always brightens up me day."

"Mine too but don't tell him I said that," Ryder said, and he tugged me back into our house.

I motioned with my hand that my lips were sealed as he closed the door behind him.

"I won't breathe a word of it," I said and placed my hand on my chest. "I promise."

"I'll hold you to that," he said, his eyes locked on mine.

The fire that ignited in his eyes told me what he wanted to do.

"I'm so happy the weather delayed us from leavin' tonight," I said as I backed away from him and removed my shoes, leaving them near the front door. "I'd have cried me heart out if I missed to-night."

I looked at my husband when he remained silent, and I laughed the second I fixated my gaze on him. He was stripping, not caring that the hall light was still on and that anyone outside could see him through the frosted glass. Granted, they wouldn't see him clearly, but still, *I* was the only person who got to experience the marvel that was his sculpted body. No one else. Ever.

"We already had sex today, Ry," I teased as I backed towards the stairs. "And Damien is home."

"He's dropping Lana home," he replied, as his trousers dropped. He stepped out of them, and it left him in just his boxer shorts. My heart skipped a beat, and my body tingled with arousal.

"You don't play fair, husband."

"Not when I want you, wife."

I swallowed. "I might be borin', though, 'cause I'm a bit tired."

"Sex with you is never boring, darling."

He says that now, but wait until I'm huge and fall asleep mid-fucking.

I waggled my brows. "You're just sayin' that 'cause you wanna get some."

"I'll get some no matter what." He smirked knowingly. "You know it, and so do I."

I scowled. "It pisses me off that you're right."

"Come on." He grinned. "Let's get you to bed. I wanna play."

The possibilities of *that* sentence kept a satisfied grin on my face way into the early hours of the morning.

CHAPTER FOUR

I had a bad feeling, but I wasn't exactly sure why I felt that way, or what could be the cause of it. I mulled over possible ideas as to why I suddenly felt like this as Ryder and I approached the absolutely *beautiful* cabin that we would be staying in for thirteen days. For a moment, the scenery distracted me from the nagging worry in my gut. All around were trees that looked as tall as the sky, every shade of green imaginable, and not a single person in sight. To me, and I'm sure to Ryder, this place was Heaven, and we hadn't even stepped out of our car to really experience it yet.

"I know that look," Ryder said from my right.

I switched my gaze to him. "What look?"

"*That* look," he said, grinning. "You've fallen in love."

My lips twitched as I turned and stared out the window as we came to a complete stop.

"Maybe," I murmured softly.

God, it's so beautiful.

"We've *got* to do this more often," I then said to Ryder as we unbuckled our seatbelts.

He laughed. "We haven't even left the car yet. There's still a big chance that you might hate it."

I snorted. "I *highly* doubt it."

"I didn't realise you'd like it out here so much," he said merrily. "You've never mentioned camping or hiking trips in your childhood, so I just assumed nature wasn't your thing."

I shrugged. "We never did anythin' like that with me parents, so I never got the urge to come into a forest, but it's gorgeous. It's so peaceful. I can't remember the last time I was somewhere this quiet but still surrounded by life."

"I know." Ryder nodded in agreement. "It's paradise."

I always thought paradise for me would be a beach—a clear blue ocean and piping hot weather—but an open forest, endless shades of green, drizzling rain, a cool breeze, and the promise of a river and lake nearby had me giddy with excitement.

"I'll grab me case and you—"

"Let me stop you right there, gorgeous," Ryder said as we got out of the car. "*I'll* get the bags while *you* carefully walk onto the porch of the cabin while we wait for the park ranger to come by and give us our key to get in."

I stared at my husband over the bonnet of our car.

"You do realise you're bein' crazy protective of me, right?"

"I'm aware of it."

I laughed. "Okay, as long as you know."

He winked and went to the back of the car to get our stuff, while I walked *carefully* to the front porch. I felt Ryder's eyes watching me as I walked, so I shouted, "Stop lookin' at me arse."

"How the hell did you know I was looking at your ass?"

"I can feel your eyes on it."

"You'll feel something else *in* it if you shake your hips one more time."

I shook them twice.

"You're gonna get it, Sweetness."

I climbed the steps off the porch and laughed when I turned and saw Ryder grab my suitcase, his duffle bag, and my side bag, and then struggled with them as he strode towards the cabin. I held my breath when he missed a step as he climbed the stairs but released it when he regained his footing.

"You *do* know there's a much easier way of doin' that, right?"

"Yes," my husband huffed, dropping the bags next to the cabin door, "but that involved two trips."

"So?"

"*So* the quicker I get you inside this cabin, the quicker your thighs spread like butter."

I slapped his shoulder. "Naughty."

"You say that like it's a bad thing."

I chuckled then turned my head to the right and watched a roughed-up Ford Kuga with mud splashed all over it drive up the roadway.

"Who is that?" I asked and pointed at the car.

"That'd be the park ranger, I assume."

Ryder moved away from me, jogged down the steps of the porch, and headed over to greet the ranger. I leaned against the door for a few minutes and only stood up straight when Ryder shook hands with the ranger in farewell. I waved at him as he got into his car and drove off down the road, getting lost in the bush only seconds later.

"We're all set," Ryder said as he wiggled the key to the cabin in my direction.

I smiled and moved aside as he climbed the steps. I gestured to the door and waited patiently for him to open it. When he did, he allowed me to walk in first, and I did so with a spring in my step. I felt like the wind was knocked out of me only seconds later.

"Ryder," I gasped. "This is *beautiful*."

"Only the best for you, darling."

I stared at the entryway with wide eyes. Stunning didn't cover it. It was incredible. The décor was like something out of an interior magazine. Everything was crafted with wood—all different shades, shapes, and varnishes stood out and got my immediate attention. I didn't feel a lick of heat, but the décor gave off a warm winter's home vibe, and I was *totally* digging it.

Without waiting for my husband, I ventured down the lengthy hallway and entered the first door on my left. It was the kitchen and sitting room combo, and it nearly knocked me off my feet. The ceilings were incredibly high with wooden beams zig-zagging from wall to wall. The paintings of breathlessly beautiful landscapes hung on the wall opposite a ten foot, in both height and width, glass window that overlooked the serene forest.

I felt like my mouth was agape from the moment I entered the cabin, but it definitely hung open when I looked to my right. The fireplace had to be the best part of what I'd seen of the house so far. It was tall, at least six foot in height, and made of solid cobblestones. The different shades of grey and navy on the stones complimented each other greatly as they scaled up the wall. Logs and blocks of coal lined the inside of the fireplace, and I couldn't wait to cuddle up next to my husband on the suede sofa that sat a metre or two away from the mouth of the fireplace.

"You like it?" my husband asked as I felt his arms come around my waist.

"Like doesn't cover it." I hummed as I placed my hands over his on my stomach. "I *love* it. This place is beautiful, Ry."

Ryder kissed my head. "I'm glad you feel that way, sweetheart. Put your feet up on the couch, and I'll get a fire going. I bet it will look great with this fireplace."

I agreed.

Ten minutes later, Ryder snuggled up next to me on the sofa as a roaring fire blazed just a couple of metres away from us. I could smell no smoke, just the clean twang of pine. I closed my eyes, and listened to the crackle and pop of the flames as they coated the pinewood and coal and turned them to ash. The sound was lulling me into a peaceful sleep—one that my husband refused me.

"Don't even *think* about napping."

I groaned as I snuggled my face into his neck and inhaled his scent.

"Nope, wake up. You have to eat before you sleep."

My belly growled in response.

"Food *does* sound good," I murmured.

"I'm glad you agree with—*Branna*."

I smiled as I nipped at Ryder's skin with my teeth before sliding my tongue over his sweet spot.

"Baby," he moaned. "Food first. Sex later."

I placed my hands on his chest and pushed him back against the cushions. I straddled his thighs before he could stop me, and I was so glad I had taken off my leggings under my dress before we sat down to cuddle. I locked my eyes on Ryder's and smiled.

"I want to play."

He swallowed. "You don't play fair."

I rolled my hips forward, feeling his growing erection under me. Ryder hissed as he brought his hands to my hips and dug his fingers into my flesh.

"Take your dress off," he almost growled.

I gripped the hem of my dress and pulled it over my head. Not a second later, I undid my bra and tossed it behind the sofa. I groaned at the freedom that no longer wearing a bra brought me, and Ryder groaned at the sight of my growing breasts. I clicked my tongue at him.

"No bitin' or suckin' on me nipples."

"What?" my husband asked. "Why not?"

"Because," I chuckled, "they're *very* tender today."

"Dammit," he grumbled.

I bit down on my lower lip and rolled my hips forward once more, but instead of a delightful ache pulsing between my thighs, I felt another sensation entirely.

"Shite," I shouted as I pushed off Ryder and ran out of the room in just my knickers.

"What's wrong?" Ryder hollered after me.

"I have to wee!" I yelled as I ran down the hallway and almost kicked open every door in sight.

I had passed by two bedrooms before I found the room I was looking for. I almost ripped my underwear off my body as I pulled them down and practically fell onto the toilet. I hated how little bladder control I had so early on in my pregnancy. I could never hold it for very long before I was pregnant, but now, I was lucky to get a minute's warning.

I flushed the toilet when I was done, and washed my hands. I glanced around the bathroom and admired the décor. Whoever designed this cabin did a hell of a job because I couldn't find a single flaw in it... until I looked into the mirror. I stared at my reflection and furrowed my brows. There were coloured streaks of lipstick on the mirror, but as I moved to get some tissue to wipe it clean, I froze. When I moved, the lipstick streaks moved with me.

"Oh my God," I breathed and looked down at my stomach.

I had a bigger bump than most women for being fifteen weeks pregnant, and I *did* already pack on twenty pounds in just a few short weeks, but I felt like I was the only person to get stretch marks so early on because it wasn't the mirror in the cabin that was flawed, it was *me*. By the base of my stomach and under my boobs, dark purple streaks appeared that I had never seen before. Thanks to the mirror, I could see the dark marks had destroyed the inside and *outside* of my thighs too.

"Fuck," I whispered.

My eyes welled with hot tears as my eyes roamed over every disgusting mark.

"Branna?"

I gasped when the handle of the bathroom door suddenly lowered.

"No!" I shouted, and grabbed for a towel on a rack next to me. "Don't come in here!"

Don't see me.

"What the hell?" Ryder said, then opened the door and quickly stepped into the room.

He looked at me then around the room then back at me.

"What's wrong with you?" he asked, frowning.

"Nothin'," I replied. "I'm just... naked."

Ryder blinked. "I've seen you naked... hundreds of times."

I felt my cheeks flush with heat.

"Yeah," I agreed, "but that was before—" I cut myself off and quickly clamped my mouth shut.

"Before what?"

Tell him.

"Nothin'." I swallowed.

"Bran," he said, his voice firm. "You're crying. What's wrong? Tell me."

I swallowed and looked away from him.

"I have stretch marks," I whispered. "Lots of them. They're on me thighs, me stomach, and even on me boobs. They're dark purple and just appeared out of nowhere. I'm sure they weren't there when I showered yesterday, and if they were, I didn't notice them."

I've seen women of all different shapes and sizes throughout different stages of their pregnancies, and the majority of them had stretch marks. Aideen even got them, but I never thought for a second how they would make me feel about my changing body. It turned out they made me feel bad.

Really bad.

"Look at me, baby," Ryder murmured.

I did, but it was during that moment that big fat tears fell from my eyes and splashed onto my cheeks.

"I love how you look, but do you think I married you because of your body?" he asked as he placed his hands on my cheeks and used his thumbs to wipe away my fallen tears.

"No," I sniffled.

My husband leaned down until his forehead touched mine. "I *love* your body, but I married you because your soul matches mine...

and because I love you more than life itself. Our looks will change over time, but our souls won't. I will always love you, and I will always want you no matter what you look like. Do you want to know why?"

I didn't *want* to know… I *needed* to know.

He reached out and gripped my towel, and I closed my eyes when he tugged on it. I released my grip and felt it fall away from my body and for cool air to quickly replace it. I gasped when I felt a fingertip gently run over my left nipple. I opened my eyes and found Ryder's gazed locked on my breasts, his hunger for me evident in his grey eyes.

"These breasts are going to feed my child," he murmured, then dropped his hand down to my thighs before slowly sliding it up to my stomach. "This body is growing my baby, and I'll be damned if you don't know how sexy that is *or* how stunningly beautiful each mark is. We created a life together, but *you* are the one who single-handedly brings that life into our world, and I will forever be in awe of you for that."

"Ryder," I rasped as more tears fell.

"They aren't stretch marks." He smiled affectionately. "They're service strips because you'll earn every single one of them growing our baby and bringing him into the world."

I laughed through my tears and threw myself at my husband, and he chuckled as he wrapped his arms tightly around me.

"I love you so much," I said into his chest.

I felt him kiss the top of my head. "I love you too, darling."

I gave him a big squeeze.

"You have made me feel *so* much better," I admitted.

"I'm glad," Ryder replied. "You should feel as beautiful as you are."

I hugged him tighter.

"You know," he murmured into my hair. "I have stretch marks too."

I pulled back with a gasp. "You lie."

"I do not." Ryder chuckled. "I have loads of them; they're just faded."

"Where are they?"

"Behind my knees, on my biceps, and on my inner thighs. I used to be really skinny when I was a kid, Bran, so when I started working out and gaining muscle, my skin stretched and I got stretch marks. It happens to everyone, not just pregnant women or people who are overweight."

"Show me," I demanded.

With a grin, Ryder's hands went to his belt buckle, and he began to undo it. He slowly, *painfully* slowly, popped the button on his jeans and lowered the zip. He pushed the jeans down to his knees and turned his leg to the right, showing me his inner thigh. I hunkered down, pushed up the hem of his briefs, and stared at Ryder's stretch marks. Granted, they were just a bit lighter than his skin colour, but he actually had them.

"How have I not noticed them before?" I murmured aloud as I used my fingertip to trace the mark.

"Because my dick is right next to them," Ryder replied nonchalantly.

I laughed and swatted at his thigh, causing him to jump back away from me.

"*Never* slap me close to my dick," he said, his tone firm. "You scared me."

I grinned as I stood up. "You're scared of me?"

"Are you kidding?" he asked, his eyes focusing on mine. "From the first moment I met you, you have *terrified* me."

"Why?" I asked, shocked.

"Because," he said with a small shrug, "I knew you were different, and I knew you had the ability to wiggle your way into my life and set up camp for the long haul."

I puffed out my chest with pride, and it caused my husband to laugh.

"I knew I'd marry you, you know?" he said softly, brushing strands of hair from my eyes. "From that first night in Darkness."

"Get out," I joked.

"I'm serious," he pressed. "It was an instant reaction that I didn't want to be without you. You made a hell of an impression, Sweetness."

"Because I had sex with you?"

"Because you stuck around *after* we had sex," Ryder clarified. "I've never had much to offer a woman other than my body, but then you came along, and you stuck around because you liked me for me, not because of my abs or face."

"Th*ey were* big sellin' points, though," I teased.

Ryder chuckled. "The abs have reduced to a four pack, and I've more lines on my face than when we first met, and you don't seem to mind."

"Sweetheart, you could be skinny as a rail or as fat as a whale, and I'd *still* get butterflies the second I saw you. I love you for *you*."

"And *that* is why you're my wife."

I looked down at our wedding bands.

"I still can't believe we're married," I said happily. "It's so surreal."

"I hope it always feels like that because I doubt I'm ever going to not be amazed that you picked me."

Before Ryder could speak another word, I got on my tiptoes and pressed my lips to his. His hands rested on my waist as he opened up to me and allowed me to take control of the kiss. I jumped when I felt his hardened length suddenly poking against my stomach.

"Ry," I said and looked down.

"That is what you do to my body," he said, and took my hand in his so he could place it over his throbbing erection. "Not pregnant Branna and pregnant Branna are *both* sexy as hell."

I laughed again. "You're worse than a teenager."

"It's not my fault my wife is hot," he countered.

I beamed up at him. "You've made me feel beautiful."

"You *are* beautiful."

I closed my hand around his erection, and it caused the hardened flesh to pulse under my grip.

"However shall I deal with this?" I said aloud.

"I'm down for *anything*," Ryder groaned as I delivered the first stroke.

I hunkered down once more. Leaning into Ryder's groin, I took the head of his cock into my mouth. My tongue swirled over the tip, and salty pre-come coated my taste buds. I took him to the back of my throat four times before I had to use my free hand to grip his thigh to avoid falling back on my arse.

"Are you—" Ryder hissed when I suckled on him but managed to finish his sentence. "Okay?"

My thighs were burning, and I could have sworn my legs began to involuntarily shake. Instead of voicing my concerns, I nodded and continued to suck on him. I pulled back for a moment just to catch my breath. It suddenly felt like my lungs were going to explode.

"Give me a second," I said.

"Are you okay?" Ryder asked, his fingers sliding into my hair.

I nodded and took a few deep breaths.

"Stand up," Ryder ordered. "You're not okay."

"I'm okay," I stressed.

"Bran, you don't have to—"

"I can do this," I angrily stated.

I looked up when Ryder laughed.

"What's funny?"

"You're arguing with me over a blow job."

I sighed, released him, and stood upright.

"I'm sorry," I said, feeling awful. "I feel weird."

"A bad weird?" he asked, worried.

"Just weird," I said with a shrug. "Really tired all of a sudden."

"Then a nap is back on the table." My husband winked as he tucked himself back inside his boxers and buttoned up his jeans. "You rest, and I'll make us dinner... once I figure out how to use the oven in the kitchen. Did you see how many dials were on that thing?"

I didn't know why, but I started to cry again, and Ryder's face lost its colour.

"Baby…" He frowned, and hugged me to him.

"I'm the worst wife," I blubbered. "I can't even give you a blow job."

"Bran." Ryder pulled back on a chuckle. "You're the best wife you can possibly be, and you're perfect at it in my book. I'm not stupid enough to think you can do things you used to before you were pregnant."

"But you didn't get to come and—"

"I'm not going to die," he cut me off. "We can fool around later in bed, but for now, let me feed my wife."

I cried harder.

"I can't stop," I sniffled.

He smiled softly. "It's your hormones."

"I hate them."

My husband guided me back into the sitting room where I sank back down onto the sofa. I calmed down enough to pick up my phone from the coffee table and check it for messages. There were none, so I held it in my hand while I stared at the flames dancing in the fireplace and let it pull me into a trance. I wasn't sure how long I stared before Ryder came and sat down next to me, gaining my attention.

"Branna." He sighed. "Why do you look like a puppy just died?"

"I just have a bad feelin' about something'," I said, feeling confused. "I don't know why, though. It's annoyin' me."

"Have you considered your sister?"

I frowned. "What about 'er?"

"Just yesterday, she was a mess over Georgie not breastfeeding anymore." Ryder winced. "She also drank herself into oblivion with Alannah."

I perked up.

"I bet you're right," I said excitedly. "I bet I'm just worried about Bronagh."

My husband raised an eyebrow. "Is there a reason you sound excited about that?"

I managed a laugh. "I'm not excited about Bronagh bein' upset or possibly dyin' of a hangover. I'm excited that nothin' else is worryin' me."

Ryder brushed a few strands of hair from my face. "What else would be bothering you?"

"I don't know." I shrugged. "And that's what bothers me. I have nothin' else to worry over, yet I still worry. Not all the time. Just sometimes. When things are feelin' too good to be true."

Ryder's features tensed a little.

"Branna," he began. "I can't convince you, given my past, but nothing else is going to happen to us. Not only have we suffered more than enough for one lifetime, but everyone who had a grudge against us is dead."

And thank God for that.

"I know that, I do. I just can't help but *expect* somethin' bad to happen."

Ryder frowned.

"You can't be blamed," he said softly. "It's not like bad things haven't happened one after the other since we met."

I hadn't meant to make him feel guilty, so I took his hands in mine and placed them on my stomach.

"Somethin' incredible has happened since we met, too."

Ryder's expression changed to one of joy.

"You're precious to me, Sweetness," he said, lifting his hands to my face. "You and our baby—you both mean life itself to me. I love you."

I placed my hands on his. "I love you, too."

He grinned. "Call your sister."

Ryder went into the kitchen and started on our dinner, while I dialled my sister's number into my phone.

"Hello?" Dominic answered on the third ring.

"Brother-in-law," I mused. "Is me sister alive?"

"Define alive?"

I grinned. "Is she breathin'?"

"Let me check... yep, she's breathing," he confirmed. "Sweating and drooling, too."

"Nice." I snorted.

"Will you *stop* shoutin', Dominic?" my sister's voice pleaded through the receiver of my phone. "Me head is goin' to explode."

"I've been whispering all morning."

"Lies," Bronagh rasped. "I heard you bangin' pots and pans for no other reason than to cause me pain."

"I was putting the dishes away."

"Yeah, right," my sister groaned. "Is there a reason you're in 'ere?"

"I wanted to ask you a question."

"Shoot."

"What's your perfect morning?" Dominic asked.

"No one talkin' to me," Bronagh replied.

"I knew you'd say that."

"Babe, I love you with me entire heart, but please, fuck off."

"Language," he teased. "Your sister is on the phone."

"Give it 'ere then," she grumbled.

I heard Dominic's chuckling then a loud, pained groan.

"You should have raised me better," Bronagh whined. "You should have preached how evil alcohol really is."

I smiled. "Would you have believed me?"

Silence.

"Probably not." My sister sighed. "Anyway, good mornin'."

"Mornin', sister dearest."

More groaning.

"I hate meself with every fibre in me body," she said softly. "I've never felt so ill in me entire life."

"If it makes you feel better, you gave me, Keela and the lads a right laugh."

"It doesn't make me feel better; it makes me feel worse."

I laughed. "Sorry."

"Are you really?"

"No." I cackled.

Bronagh began to laugh but quickly groaned in pain.

"Dominic," she called. "Can you get me a painkiller?"

"Two pills and a glass of water are already on your nightstand."

"Oh," Bronagh replied. "I love you."

"I know," came his response.

"Aw," I cooed. "How sweet."

"Shut up," she grumbled. "These tablets better take me head-ache away before I cry me eyes out."

I waited until she took her painkillers and rehydrated herself.

She smacked her lips together and said, "That water was the nicest thing I've ever swallowed."

Don't let Dominic hear you say that.

I shook my head. "I'm sure it was."

"I've either had the worst nightmare ever, or they're flashbacks from last night. I'm seriously prayin' for the former."

"Fire some of them at me, and I'll let you know."

"Karaoke with Lana."

"Flashback."

"Almost getting kicked out of the pub for strippin'."

"Flashback."

"Dancing on the stage."

"Flashback."

"Kissin' Lana."

"Nightmare... I think."

"Oh, my *God*." Bronagh groaned.

I chuckled.

"I don't know why I've done this to meself."

"I do. You were sad over Georgie possibly self-weanin'."

"She's definitely weanin'," Bronagh mumbled. "She drank a full eight-ounce bottle last night and slept through the night for the first time ever. She had another bottle this morning and some pureed breakfast, Dominic said." My sister sighed. "I held 'er on me chest and she didn't even hint for me boob. I still can't believe it."

"I know, kid, but it'll get easier for you."

"I hope so because I feel pretty damn useless right about now."

"You still have to do everythin' you've been doin' for her but just usin' a bottle and a spoon now."

"I guess," Bronagh mumbled.

"Want to hear somethin' shitty about *my* day?" I offered.

"Of course," came my sister's immediate response.

I chuckled. "Guess who discovered a billion purple stretch marks on 'er body?"

My sister winced. "It's that bad?"

"It's like a roadmap to hell, and I'm only in me second tri-mester."

Bronagh laughed. "You're probably bein' dramatic."

"No, Bee, seriously, they're everywhere."

"Well, they'll fade eventually, if it's any consolation?"

"It is," I said. "Ten minutes ago I'd have told you to shove that consolation up your arse, but me fabulous husband made me feel beautiful —"

"I am possibly dyin' of a hangover, so the last thing I need to think of is me brother-in-law doin' the nasty to me big sister."

I burst into laughter. "Chill, we didn't get that far. I had to wee, and the mood was killed."

"The joys of pregnancy." My sister snorted.

I smiled. "I'll let you go so you can die in peace."

"Wait," she said quickly. "Are you and Ry at the cabin yet?"

"We are, and it's stunnin'." I beamed. "It's perfect."

"Take loads of pictures," my sister reminded.

"I will."

"Enjoy it, you and Ry deserve the best honeymoon possible."

My heart fluttered. "Thanks, baby."

"I'll call you later if I haven't already passed on to me next life."

I laughed. "Bye, crazy."

When I hung up with Bronagh, I stood up and joined Ryder in the kitchen. He had figured out how to turn the oven on, I could feel the slight heat coming from it as it began to preheat. I nudged my way onto a stool, leaned my elbows on the island countertop, and stared at Ryder as he began chopping up vegetables.

"I got the food we bought out of the car while you were on the phone," he said, and gestured to the food he was dicing. "How is Bee doing?"

"She claims she's dyin'."

Ryder snorted. "Not surprising, considering how drunk you said she was."

I nodded in agreement.

"Alannah is probably just as miserable."

I snorted. "I'll call 'er later to see."

Ryder's lips quirked.

"I wonder how Aideen is," I said, voicing my thoughts.

Ryder looked at me intently.

"What?" I asked.

He shrugged. "I'm thinking that coming away while Aideen is so close to birthing this baby was a bad idea."

"Why a bad idea?"

"Because..." My husband sighed. "What if she has the baby tonight? Would you be okay with waiting nearly *two weeks* to meet the kid?"

No.

"Yes."

Ryder laughed. "You're a terrible liar."

My lips twitched.

"Okay," I conceded. "I wouldn't exactly be jumpin' for joy at havin' to wait so long, but this is our *honeymoon*. She knows she'll be in good hands with Ash and Sally. I wouldn't want to leave 'ere if it can be helped."

Ryder smiled, satisfied with my reply.

"Let's hope Aideen holds it together a little while longer," he said, his tone hopeful.

I smirked. "I'm gonna tell her you wished for her to go over-due."

"Evil wench!" he hissed.

I erupted with laughter when he snaked his way behind me and tickled up and down my sides.

"Mercy," I pleaded, cackling like a mad woman.

My husband relented. "I love you."

I leaned back against his chest. "I love you, too."

He kissed my shoulder then went back to cooking.

"What can I do to help?" I asked.

"You can just sit there and let me look at you."

I snorted but did as asked and remained seated.

"You know Alec got a job at the animal shelter he volunteers at a couple of times a week?" Ryder said, bringing a huge smile to my face.

"No way!" I exclaimed.

"Yep, they offered him a full-time job. He starts tomorrow."

My stomach flipped with excitement.

"I'm so happy for 'im," I gushed. "I know you're all strugglin' over what to do for work now that you're all straight laced."

"Don't tell Bronagh, but Dominic is applying for a full-time po-sition in the new leisure centre that's opening next month. The gym they have there is supposed to be huge. He loved working privately with his clients, but the money is better at the centre, and it's a fixed paycheck so he doesn't have to worry about not having enough money for bills and food week to week."

"That's amazin', but why hasn't he told Bronagh?"

"He didn't want to get her hopes up. She knows he only fought under Brandon Daley to help get info for me when the feds were breathing down my neck, but she isn't convinced he is done with that part of his life."

I nodded my head in understanding.

"I hope he gets it," I said. "I'll pray every night."

Ryder was quiet for a moment then said, "It's got me thinking about what I'm going to do for work. Especially now that we're married and you're pregnant."

"Do you have an idea of what you *want* to do?"

I didn't want him taking a job just for the sake of a wage because he'd be miserable if he did that.

"My options are limited because I've no schooling or college qualifications behind me, but I don't *want* to do the back to education thing. I wouldn't have the patience for it. Kane mentioned to me that Aideen's father is looking for a few drivers for tows and roadside rescue now that they've moved to a bigger auto shop and expanded the business. He put in a good word for me, and Mr Collins wants to meet with me when we're back from our honeymoon. I like cars, and Aideen's brothers are cool since we sorted our differences. It might be a good fit."

My heart fluttered.

"That is the best thing I've heard all day, baby."

Ryder smiled. "I'm excited about it. I can't wait to take care of you."

"Honey." I frowned. "You do take care of me."

"You pay our bills, Branna."

I chuckled. "It's not the 1940s. Women are capable of workin' and supportin' their families."

Ryder snorted. "I know that, and I love you for it, but I'm a provider. It makes me feel less than a man when I can't pay our bills, buy our groceries, or get you flowers whenever I want, but it's going to change. Soon. I promise."

"I trust you," I said. "With me life."

Ryder smiled and continued to prepare our dinner.

"And FYI, if you're goin' to buy me somethin', make it choco-lates instead of flowers."

My husband joyfully laughed. "Noted."

Ryder's laughter, his plans for the future, and his love for me pushed back my nagging thoughts and focused my mind on the now. This was what my happiness was all about. He made everything bet-ter. No matter how bad things got I knew when I looked at my side, I would find him there.

CHAPTER FIVE

When I awoke on the tenth morning of our honeymoon, I found myself wishing we had just arrived. I couldn't wait to see my family when we returned home, but this private time away with Ryder had done us a world of good. I was more in love with him than ever before, and to be honest, I didn't think I had ever had as many orgasms in my life. If I hadn't known Ryder was a selfless lover before were arrived at our little cabin, I damn well knew after our sex marathon.

A marathon that I was *still* in the running for.

I felt bad that Ryder was catering to me and making me feel on top of the world during most of the time we had sex. Blow jobs were pretty much out of the question in my current state of pregnancy, which *sucked*—no pun intended. Whenever I gave him one, my breathing would labour, and I'd develop a stitch in my side that would halt sexy time until it passed. He said it didn't matter, but it did to me. I hated being limited to what I could do to pleasure him. I dreaded to think how much of a sex vegetable I'd become further along into my pregnancy.

I shivered with fright as that was *definitely* not something I was looking forward to.

A snap, crackle, and pop drew my attention to the right of the room. I lifted my head and smiled when I saw the fireplace was alive and dancing with flames. Ryder must have awoken during the early hours of the morning and repacked the fire with logs. I was greatly appreciative of it, having learned a few days ago what it felt like to wake up to a freezing cold room. I rested my head back against my pillow, smiling as waves of heat floated over the bed. I was the most comfortable and content that I had been in a long time, and when I looked to my left, it became concrete in my mind that this moment—this feeling—I experienced when I looked at my husband would be forever planted in my memory.

I loved him more than a person could love another, and I knew how lucky I was to have him.

I turned onto my left side, and for a few minutes, I watched him sleep. I smiled every so often when his snoring would disturb his sleep, and he pulled a funny face until he settled back into his slumber. When I was sure he wasn't going to wake up, I lifted my hand to his face and traced his defined jawline with my fingertips. I slid my fingers down his neck and onto his chest where I played with the hair my fingers skimmed over. His torso was exposed, but a blanket covered his lower half. I traced his abdominal muscles and noted only four of them were defined where there used to be six.

Ryder had commented on his loss of muscle and added lines to his face when I discovered my stretch marks when we first arrived at the cabin. I felt horrible about them, and I worried Ryder would view me as I viewed myself. When I expressed that, he expressed how different he looked since we first met and listed the changes in his body. I realised then that the slight changes in his body never affected how much I loved him. He was still incredibly sexy and had the best body I'd ever seen. I knew his younger brothers were ripped and defined beyond anything, but I couldn't explain it. When I thought of the perfect body—the perfect man—I saw Ryder.

No one could compare to him, and no one ever would.

I knew then that my gaining weight, having stretch marks, and eventually having a basketball for a stomach wouldn't change how Ryder perceived me. I was beautiful to him before, I was beautiful to him now, and I'd still be beautiful to him after I had our baby. His confidence in me gave me the confidence I needed and greatly appreciated.

"You're perfect," I whispered to his sleeping form.

He didn't wake, but he did stir. He moved his legs, and it tugged the blanket that covered him further down his thighs. My husband, as always, slept naked as the day he was born, and I had zero problems with it. My hand, still on his stomach, continued to trace his abs. I quietly chuckled when I noticed the beginnings of morning wood. I shook my head, amused that even in a dead sleep men could get hard. I looked at Ryder's face as I slid my hand down to his groin and took his cock in my hand.

I lightly squeezed it, and Ryder's lips parted. His hips also involuntarily twitched upward ever so slightly. I positioned my hand correctly and began to stroke up and down. It didn't take longer than twenty or so seconds for Ryder's muscles to tense and for soft moans to escape him. I leaned in to place my lips on his neck and kiss him softly. I dragged my tongue over his sweet spot, nipped at his flesh with my teeth, and squeezed him at the same time, causing him to hiss. I pulled back and looked at his face, watching the moment he awoke.

"Oh, shit," he rasped, his voice husky.

Without a word, I placed my mouth on my husband's, enjoying his surprise to my playtime with him. I smiled against his lips when his right hand fisted my hair, and his tongue forced his way past my lips. I yelped and pulled back from our kiss when he bit my lower lip. I released his cock and brought my hand to my mouth.

"Ow!"

"You cheated," Ryder said, a little breathless. "I said *you* were to always come first, and if you kept doing what you were doing, I was going to bust all over your hand."

I pushed myself upright and turned, letting my legs dangle over the side of the bed.

"That was kind of the idea, you shithead," I huffed.

I was about to stand up, but before I could even move, Ryder's hands were on my shoulders, and he applied enough pressure to keep my arse on the mattress. I shivered when I felt his thighs press firmly against my back, along with something else that was hard. I opened my mouth to speak but moaned when Ryder's tongue slid over the flesh on my neck before he grazed my shoulder with his teeth.

"I've got chills," I murmured.

"They're multiplying," Ryder finished.

I closed my eyes and laughed. "Keep doin' what you're doin', Danny boy."

My husband kissed the back of my head as he chuckled to himself. His hands moved to my shoulders, and he began a gentle massage that made my toes curl. Once or twice, I moaned out loud, and I felt Ryder's cock twitch against my back, but he didn't comment on it; he just kept doing what he was doing.

"This mornin' was supposed to be about *me* makin' *you* feel good," I said softly, hissing in delight a little when he'd knead out a knot.

"Making you feel good *does* make me feel good," Ryder replied.

It was hard to argue with that logic, but I argued anyway.

"Ryder."

"Branna."

"I'm not jokin'."

"Do you hear me laughing?"

I opened my eyes. "Let me give you a hand job, for God's sake."

"Well, if it's for God's sake."

I smiled. "I hate you."

Ryder moved his lips to my ear. "We both know that's a *lie*."

"I'm not so sure," I baited.

I gasped when I was tugged back farther onto the bed and found myself on my back and staring up at the ceiling. I smiled when my thighs were parted, and Ryder wiggled his way up my body until his face came into view above me. He was in the push-up position, his hands on either side of my shoulders, and even though he held himself off me, he lowered his torso, so his stomach brushed mine.

"I used to be able to lie on you in his position, holding myself up with just my elbows."

I snorted. "You should have thought about that *before* you knocked me up."

Ryder smirked. "I'll be able to do it again in a few months."

Literally a *few* months.

I squealed. "We're goin' to be *parents* and have a little mini-us!"

My husband only smiled at my excitement before he disappeared. He kissed his way down my body, and I couldn't help but giggle when I became ticklish. I attempted to sit up, but then my nightdress was pushed up, and I felt a hot breath on my inner thighs.

"Ryder." I chuckled. "I'm not even in the mood for—omigod."

Without warning, my husband's lips fastened on my clit, and he suckled on it until spasms of pleasure fluttered to life. I pressed my head back into the mattress and thrust my pelvis into Ryder's face, causing him to groan against me. He hooked his arms around my thighs and kept my arse on the bed as he feasted on me.

"Ryder," I moaned. "Circles, baby. Move your tongue in—Holy Christ!"

He rotated his tongue in *lazy* circles, and the sweet torture sent chills through my body. I badly wanted to reach down and fist his hair in my hands. Even though my bump wasn't big, I didn't want to have to bend forward to do it, so I settled on gripping the bed sheets for dear life. My moans became audible and so did my breathing. My chest began to hurt as I sucked air into my lungs. It wasn't an agonising pain; it felt more like a stitch, but it was enough to take centre stage over my pleasure.

"Ryder." I winced. "Stop."

Almost instantly, Ryder was sitting up, resting back on his heels with his hands on my bent knees.

"What's wrong?" he asked.

I whimpered. "I've a stitch in me side. It hurts."

He quickly got up from the bed and helped me to sit upright then fully stand up off the bed. I closed my eyes and took slow, deep breaths while holding onto Ryder's biceps, and then, out of nowhere, when the pain subsided, I began to cry.

"Bran?" Ryder said, alarmed.

"I'm the worst... partner... ever," I sobbed. "I can't even do se- sex good an-anymore."

I thought I heard him chuckle as he folded his arms around my body and kissed the crown of my head. He held me, naked as a baby, and swayed me side to side until my sobs became sniffles and my sniffles became sighs.

"I love you," I said to him, "but you have to be gettin' sick of this. Because I am."

"I'll never get sick of you."

I sat back on our bed while Ryder got dressed. I watched as he pulled on his boxer briefs, his socks, and then his grey trousers—that he insisted I call 'sweats'. But I just couldn't call them anything other than what they were—trousers.

"This should be your outfit every day," I said, eyeing his body up with nothing but love, admiration and a hell of a lot of lust.

Ryder looked at me and saw me checking him out. His lips twitched, humour tracing his features.

"I'm not fully dressed yet," he commented.

I locked my eyes on his torso.

"I'm *very* happy with you bein' topless."

Ryder laughed as he pulled on a plain white t-shirt.

"If we lived in Hawaii, I would, but we live in Ireland... and it's winter."

I smiled. "God loves a trier, and I had to try."

My husband smiled, shaking his head before he rounded the bed and held his hand out to me.

"Let's go get you fed, and then we can go for a walk."

I saluted. "Yes, sir."

He cocked an eyebrow. "Say that again."

His voice was husky, and his eyes were hooded.

I grinned and shook my head. "Get your mind out of the gutter."

"Your body is on my mind, and that is the furthest thing from the gutter."

I took his extended hand. "Charmer."

"If being honest makes me charming, then so be it," Ryder teased.

We ventured off into the kitchen, and after forty minutes, both of our hunger was sated. We spent a further ten minutes arguing about my outfit choice. I aimed for comfort; Ryder aimed for temperature and weather-appropriate attire. He won by a landslide, simply because I didn't have the energy to argue with him. When we both were suited and booted, we headed outside to the well-marked trail facing the cabin.

The trees over our heads folded over one another and almost formed a tunnel of sorts, making the path we were walking down hand in hand shaded and murky. It was beautiful and made it feel like we were going on a secret adventure. I had a little spring to my step with this thought, and my husband was quick to put me in line.

"Watch your step," Ryder said, his hold tightening on me.

I did as asked, and made sure I placed my feet on solid ground and not slippery leaves. It was a little difficult since the leaves were everywhere. They were every shade of orange and red imaginable, but even their allure could not hide the fact that they were slippery little death traps. When I was sure of my footing, I lifted my head and looked at the natural beauty that surrounded me.

"It's so beautiful here."

Ryder squeezed my hand. "I agree... In fact, it's so beautiful I want a picture of it."

I stopped walking when he did, and shoved my hands into my pockets when he reached into his own for his phone. I raised my brows when he started to back up. I made a move to walk with him, but he held up his hands.

"No," he said. "I want a picture of what's beautiful. You."

I blushed like a schoolgirl.

"I've still got it," Ryder said as he patted himself on the back.

"Are you sure you can see the background or do I take up all the space?" I asked, grinning.

Ryder snorted. "*Please*, you're an itty bitty thing."

I laughed. "I wish."

My husband simply smiled as he lifted his phone and pointed it in my direction. I turned a little to the side, placed my hands on my bump in a way that showed I was cradling the little bundle of joy inside me, and beamed a smile when Ryder counted to three.

He wolf-whistled when he took the picture and said, "Damn, my wife is sexy."

"Kiss arse."

"*Can* I kiss your ass?"

I laughed. "If you want to, you can."

"Oh." Ryder grinned as he pocketed his phone. "I want to."

He began to advance on me, and I instantly began to screech.

"Stop," I squealed with laughter. "I can't run!"

"You're easy prey for me then, Sweetness," Ryder joked as he jumped for me and captured my lips the instant his body touched mine.

I laughed against his lips and flung my arms around his neck, pulling him as close as possible to me. He made that almost animalistic growling sound in the back of his throat like he always did when his body reacted to mine. I hummed as I kissed his lips, before nipping at his lower lip with my teeth.

"It's colder than a witch's tit out here," he warned. "Don't start something we can't finish right now."

I smiled as I released his lip. Ryder's eyes held a heated promise of what later would bring, but for the moment, he wanted us to focus on our mini walking adventure, which was what we did. After a blissful hour of exploring, a sudden rumble of thunder startled us both. I looked up, and just beyond the mountains, were nasty looking clouds that were rolling in. Ryder checked the weather app on his phone and cursed under his breath just as lightening *cracked* and flashed across the sky.

"A storm is coming.".

We decided we'd had enough nature for one day with the weather warning and headed back to the warm and toasty cabin. We made it inside, and not a second later, my phone rang from the bedroom.

I did a mixture of a brisk walk and a waddle, according to Ryder, which caused me to give him the finger as I headed towards the bedroom with his laughter flowing behind me. I grabbed my phone from the nightstand, glanced at the screen, and then answered the call as I placed it against my ear.

"Hey, Kay, what's up?"

"Aideen had 'er baby!" Keela's excited voice squealed through the receiver of my phone.

"What?" I gasped. "She went early *again?*"

"Yep, but it took longer than Jax this time around."

"What do you mean?"

"She went into labour yesterday and only had 'im ten minutes ago. She held out until late last night before she went to the hospital."

I furrowed my brows and startled once again when thunder boomed outside.

"Why didn't anyone ring me?" I asked, focusing on the phone call.

"That was Ado's call," Keela said quickly. "She didn't want to interrupt your honeymoon."

"Is she shittin' me?" I asked, exasperated.

"I know. We told 'er you and Ry would want to know, but she made us all promise to wait until she gave birth before we called. And by promise, I mean she threatened us all to within an inch of our lives."

I shook my head. "I'm goin' to beat 'er arse."

Keela snorted. "She's doin' great and so is your new *nephew*."

Nephew.

"She had *another* boy?"

"Yeah," Keela squealed again. "He weighed ten pounds, four ounces and is twenty-one inches long. He is a *big* boy. They called him Locke Ryder Slater!"

Locke Ryder Slater.

I began jumping up and down—as best as I could—with joy, but stopped almost instantly when loud rain began to belt against the bedroom window. The sun was setting, and blackened clouds were quickly shutting out any orange glow with murky shade. I frowned at the forest our cabin overlooked. The wind had picked up considerably and was causing the trees to thrash from side to side.

"Bran? Can... hear... me... you... Hello?"

"Keela? You're breakin' up, babe."

"Can you hear me?" she asked loudly.

"Yeah," I said, raising my voice, too. "Sorry, the weather is gettin' bad up 'ere. Ryder said a storm is comin' in."

"That's one of the reasons I called," Keela replied as I turned on our bedroom light. "Heavy rain, thunder and lightnin', and gale force winds are expected. We're gettin' the tail end of Storm Harry that hit the UK last night."

Well, fuck.

"Hopefully it'll pass soon," I said.

"Branna? Can... Me... Branna? Hello?"

"I can't hear you."

"Call... later. Hello?"

"Okay, babe. Talk to you later."

The reception had been so shitty whenever my sister or friends called over the last few days, but it was really bad now that a storm was rolling in. It was another reason I was excited to get home. I couldn't wait to have a real chat with them without being cut off.

"Ryder!" I hollered when I hung up my phone. "Ryder, quick,

come 'ere!"

"Branna?" I heard my husband roar in response. "I'm coming!"

I heard his feet pounding against the floorboards as he ran down the hallway. I jumped when the door to our room flew open and crashed into the wall with a resounding bang.

"What's wrong?" my husband asked, his eyes wild.

"Aideen had the baby!"

"For fuck's sake!" He breathed and place his hand on his chest. "You scared the shit out of me. I thought something was wrong with you, Branna."

Fuck.

I winced. "I'm sorry, I forgot."

He closed his eyes for a few seconds then reopened them.

"Is Ado and the baby okay?" he asked, dropping his hand to his side. "Everything went like it was supposed to?"

I nodded. "Aideen is doin' great and so is our new *nephew*."

"Another boy?" He laughed, his worry for me easing from his face. "I bet Kane is *loving* that."

"I'm sure he is." I chuckled. "Ring 'im, I'm sure he'll want to hear from you. Just don't be surprised if you get cut off, the storm messed up me call with Keela."

Ryder did just that. He gave me one more once-over, and when he was sure I was okay, he took out his phone, tapped on the screen, and pressed it against his ear.

"Kane?" he said, smiling wide when his brother answered. "Bro, congratulations to you and Ado. Another boy! I'm so happy for you both."

Ryder laughed at something Kane said, then replied, "Ah, it could have been worse. You could have almost missed the birth like when Jax was born."

I could practically hear Kane's, "Fuck you," from across the room. I smiled when Ryder laughed once more, but smiled wider when he got very quiet very fast.

"Say that again," my husband requested. "I think I'm losing

you. It sounded like you said his name is Locke *Ryder*."

He did say that.

My heart warmed when Ryder began to shuffle a little from side to side.

"Kane, I don't know what to say other than I'm honoured."

They spent a minute or two on the phone after that, and when the reception went shitty, Ryder hung up.

He looked at me and said, "They gave him my name."

"Isn't that brilliant?"

"Yeah," he said, clearing his throat. "Brilliant."

Butterflies exploded in my stomach when he rubbed his eyes.

"Are you goin' to cry?" I asked, smiling so wide my cheeks began to hurt.

"No," he said quickly. "I just have something in my eyes. You were right about it being a little dusty in here."

"Yeah," I teased. "It must be the dust because you'd *never* cry over your little brother given his newborn son *your* name."

"Of course not," my husband countered. "It's not a big deal."

"Yep," I deadpanned. "Not a big deal at all."

Ryder sniffled and rubbed his eyes again.

"I'm going to the restroom," he managed to get out before he turned and fled the room.

I covered up my giggles because I knew he was going to unleash his 'man emotions' when I wasn't around. All men were supposed to follow that code, according to the brothers. Never 'pussy out' and cry in front of anyone. The Man Bible had a whole chapter on it—or that was what Dominic said anyway. That damn code they lived by would soon change once they all had children, and they watched them grow. I'd bet my life on it.

That evening, when I emerged from my nap—that was really like a six-hour coma—I found Ryder in the kitchen cooking us dinner. He hadn't spotted me yet, so I quietly walked into the room and simply watched the magnificence that was my husband.

I leaned against the kitchen counter and rubbed my belly when the baby kicked.

"The little one is active today," I said.

Ryder looked up, smiled, and then rounded the counter to kiss me in greeting.

"Sleep well?" he asked.

"So well," I purred, shaking out my relaxed limbs.

He chuckled as he moved back to the stove. The baby kicked hard. Again.

"I bet this baby will look like you," I murmured aloud.

Ryder looked up at me and winked. "We'll eventually have one that will resemble you more than me, so don't give up hope."

I snorted. "How many kids are you plannin' on us havin'?"

Ryder said, "Five."

Lord.

I rested my cheek on my hand. "You're still set on that, huh?"

"Of course," he said. "I've always been set on it."

I tilted my head to the side. "What if I only want one?"

"Why would you only want one baby?" he asked, his tone sounded baffled.

"Because some people are happy with one," I stated.

"But will the child be happy?" my husband questioned as he continued to cook our steaks. "An only child is a lonely child."

I rolled my eyes.

"Our baby has *three* cousins so far that won't be much older. He or she will have plenty of interaction with other children."

"How do you know?" Ryder quizzed as he flipped the steaks that sizzled in the pan. "How do you know that my brothers and the girls won't move someplace else, and we won't see them as much?"

My heart began to pound against my chest.

"They won't move," I answered.

"You don't know that," Ryder said as he sprinkled some seasoning into the pan. "For all we know, they might want to move over the north side of the city or to a different county with better schools for their kids. I doubt they'd stay here just to give our kid some company."

I never thought of anything like that. I guess I always assumed we would all remain living close to one another. The sudden thought of my sister, friends, and Ryder's brothers not being nearby didn't sit well with me, and I was suddenly pissed with Ryder for putting that worry in my head.

I stared at him. "Why are you bein' so negative about this?"

"I'm not." He sighed. "I just don't want you to assume that our niece and nephews will compensate for brothers and sisters to our baby."

"You'd say mass just so I'll agree with you on havin' five kids."

"What does that even mean?" he questioned.

"It means," I said firmly, "that you'd say anythin' to get what you want."

Ryder snorted, and it was at that moment that I knew he wasn't going to acquiesce to this no matter what I said, and it was beginning to drive me insane.

"What if I can't have any more?"

Ryder turned off the stove and served our steaks and sides onto plates.

"That's crazy talk," he said, dismissing my question.

"No, it's not," I stated, not liking that this conversation was quickly turning into an argument. "What if the baby I'm carryin' is the only one I'll *ever* carry? Will he or she not be enough because there are no other siblings?"

Ryder looked up at me and paled. "No, of course not—"

"Then *why* are you makin' such a big deal out of this?" I demanded. "*Why* are you fightin' me on this? Why do you need four more kids? *Why?*"

"Branna, listen—"

"No, *you* listen." My voice suddenly breaking. "I had me choices taken away from me before, and I refuse to have them taken away again. If I don't want more kids, then I'm not havin' more. It's *my* body. That's the end of this conversation!"

I wish I'd spoken with assertiveness and had my head held high, but big fat tears were falling from my eyes, and I was sniffling like crazy. I might have looked like a mess, but I said my piece and got my point across, and that was the important thing.

"Now, if you don't mind," I hiccupped. "I'm goin' outside for some fresh air."

"Branna, I'm so sor—"

"Don't be sorry." I cut him off. "Be mindful of me feelins' and understandin' of me decisions. You don't have to like them, but you damn well better respect them. I'm your wife; your utmost respect should *be* for me."

I left the kitchen without waiting for Ryder's reply and headed outside to the front porch. I shivered the moment I closed the front door behind me. The rain had lessened slightly, but frigid cold nipped at me and caused goose bumps to break out on my flushed skin. My annoyance forced my legs to move, and without realising it, I headed in the direction of the trail Ryder and I had walked on daily. The trees overhead provided some protection against the falling rain.

I only walked a few minutes or so before a noisy squeal got my attention.

I scanned the darkened bush and jumped when I heard the squeal again. I squinted my eyes, and I walked forward. I heard the rush of running water and knew the river was nearby. I pushed through some trees until I came close to the embankment of the river that ran through the forest. It wasn't full dark outside, but it wouldn't be long until I couldn't see my hand in front of my face. I knew I needed to go back to the safety of the cabin, but I couldn't leave the animal that was hurting. I tried to turn around, but my conscience wouldn't allow me to do so. The screech of pain was louder this time, and I gasped when I found what was making the awful sounds.

"Oh, baby," I whispered as I stared down at a small rabbit that had somehow got its foot tangled in some plastic that was caught on some fallen branches.

I looked around for something to cut the plastic, but the best thing I could find was a semi-sharp rock.

"Shhh," I cooed to the rabbit, hoping to offer it some comfort.

I bent down on my knees and took hold of the little being. I tried to apply some strength to keep it still, but it was useless, so I put up with the flying paws and kicking legs as I began to untangle the lengthy piece of plastic from around the animal's small leg. When nothing could be untangled further, I used the rock to saw through the material until it snapped and the animal was freed.

The rabbit kicked me the second it was free.

"You ungrateful little shite!" I exclaimed.

He began to move away slowly before darting off into the bushes and disappearing.

"You're welcome, Bugs!" I yelled after it, chuckling a little.

A gust of wind hit my back and caused me to shiver. I placed my dirty hands on my thighs and rubbed them against the fabric of my leggings. I shivered a little as the breeze cut through me, and I flinched when thunder roared across the Heavens. I pushed myself upwards, but before I got a solid footing on the ground, my left foot slipped from underneath me thanks to the soaking wet leaves that scattered my surroundings.

"Branna?" Ryder's voice called from behind me.

He sounded a bit of a distance away, and I imagined him standing on the front porch of the cabin looking for me.

"Ryder!" I screamed just as I fell forward.

I hit the ground hard, left shoulder first, and then awkwardly and painfully began to slide down the embankment. It all happened rapidly fast. One moment I was falling, then I was airborne, and the next second, I was submerged under a body of freezing water. My eyes were open, but all I could see was mass darkness.

That darkness had hold of me and put up a fight to keep me in its grasp.

CHAPTER SIX

Water.

I was *under*water.

The cold stabbed my skin like tiny pinpricked needles. Water and debris cloaked me, and what felt like the longest few seconds of my life quickly became the hardest and most painful. I kicked my legs and used my arms to slice through the water in an effort to thrust myself to the surface, but it quickly became apparent that the current had a firm hold and wasn't letting go anytime soon.

It was then that a fire ignited in the centre of my chest, and almost instantly spread to my aching lungs. It was ironic that being under a pool of ice-cold water awakened a burning fire within me. It was as if I could hear my lungs screaming until it registered in my mind that it wasn't my lungs screaming, it was me. When my lungs were spent of oxygen, silence wrapped its arms around me, and with the company of the swaying current, it began to lull me to sleep.

I was being swallowed whole by darkness, and I was acutely aware of it.

Ryder took centre stage in my mind. Flashes from the moment I met him were replaced with images from throughout our years together. They flicked through my mind like a high-speed slideshow. It slowed down at our wedding day, and once more, my heart swelled as he made his vows to me, declared his love for me, and later made me his forever. Fast forward to seeing his face when I informed him that he was going to be a father to our baby.

My husband. Our baby. My sister. My family. My life.

I looked upwards and was surprised to see light within the darkness. Each one of those I loved had me using the last of my strength to reach up to the rippled light that shone above me. Something hard struck my palm, so I latched onto it. I felt myself being pulled to a stop as the current rushed around me. I gripped the object and heaved myself upwards, and the second I broke the surface, I began to choke. I coughed, spluttered, and greedily sucked oxygen into my inflamed lungs. I used my free hand to grab what felt like a log or a large tree branch.

I pulled myself onto the bank of the river, I put all of my weight onto the sopping wet log, and just when I was about to breathe a sigh of relief for making it onto solid ground, disaster struck. Literally. I screamed as the log that saved me snapped in two and fell on me. It landed on my left leg and pinned it to the freezing cold, wet, muddy ground.

My heart slammed into my chest, and I began to cry, not being able to believe what had just happened and how bad the situation was that I had found myself in. I felt the pain of a stitch in my side as I continued to breathe heavily, but nothing compared to the sickening feeling that took up residence in my belly.

I placed my hands over my abdomen and said, "Please kick."

Nothing.

"Please," I whispered. "Please move for Mammy."

The baby had kicked not ten minutes ago inside the cabin, but I had a stomach churning feeling that something could be wrong after what had just happened to me. I looked up at the starlit sky as I cried.

"Please, God," I pleaded. "Don't take me baby from me."

I expected only silence, but faintly, I heard a familiar voice call out... my name.

Ryder.

"Help me!" I shouted.

I heard his voice get louder, and I heard the rustle of branches and the snap of twigs.

"Branna!"

Oh, thank God.

"Ryder!" I screamed with relief. "I'm down 'ere!"

"Keep talking to me," he shouted as heavy rain began to fall. "I can't see a damn thing."

It had gotten considerably darker in just a few minutes and made it almost impossible to make out anything against the darkened bush.

"I'm stuck," I called out to him. "I fell do-down the bank and in-to the wa-water. I got out of the water, but when I pu-pulled meself out, the branch I used as an an-anchor broke free and fell on me leg. It's too he-heavy to move, and the water is risin'."

It was rising *fast*.

The hard rain that had fallen for the last thirty minutes was too much for the small river to contain, resulting in it rushing over the banks.

"Are you hurt bad?" Ryder asked; panic laced around his words as he neared me.

"I'm okay, I th-think," I said through chattering teeth. "It's just me leg that hu-hurts."

I heard him curse a few times, and I screamed when something squeaked and ran over my legs.

"What is it?" Ryder shouted.

"A rat," I cried out. "Oh, God, I think a rat ju-just ran ov-over me legs!"

I was *terrified* of rats.

"I'm coming, baby, I'm coming."

Ten seconds later, I heard the bushes next to me rustle before my husband pushed through them.

"Bran," he breathed, a sigh of relief escaping him as he dropped to his knees next to me.

He felt down my body until his hands encountered the log that pinned me. He got to his feet, bent down, gripped the log, and with a grunt, he lifted it enough that I could pull my leg free. It throbbed with pain, but I could bend my knee, and that removed any lingering fear that it may have been broken.

"Ryder," I said, gaining his attention. "I haven't felt the baby move si-since I left the ho-house. I don't know how long I was un-under the water for."

I couldn't see his face clearly, but I heard his sharp intake of breath.

"The hospital," he breathed. "We'll go back to the cabin, get you dry and warm, and then we'll drive to the hospital. We'll make it there in a few hours, okay?"

"Okay," I replied, still crying.

Ryder's hold on me tightened. "He's okay."

Sobs wracked through me.

"What if he's not?" I asked, using a gender term for the first time since I found out I was pregnant. "What if I've ki-killed 'im? Oh, God, he ca-can't be dead, Ryder. He ca-can't be."

"He. Is. Okay," my husband said firmly as he bent down and lifted me into his arms bridal style.

It didn't take very long for us to get back to the cabin, and the heat that hit me upon entering the haven was like Heaven.

"We ne-need to g-go," I demanded as we entered the bathroom.

Ryder stripped me of my wet clothes and put me in the shower. Without warning, he turned on the water. I gasped with shock and pressed my body to his. The water felt boiling hot, and my skin screamed in protest.

"Too hot!" I screeched.

Ryder held me in place.

"It's lukewarm," he assured me. "Just give your body a chance to get used to it. We need to get your temperature up before I get you dry, baby. The last thing you need is a fever."

I rested my head on his chest and closed my eyes. My limbs were still shaking of their own accord, but the water did begin to feel beautifully warm instead of shockingly hot, and my body almost instantly relaxed.

"No," Ryder suddenly snapped and shook me. "Stay awake. Move your arms and legs around to generate heat."

"I'm so sorry," I whimpered and tried to do as he asked.

My husband squeezed me tightly. "Stop. It's fine. You're fine, the baby is fine. Everything is fine."

Everything wasn't fine, and he knew it.

"F-forgive me," I pleaded. "Please, forgive—"

"*Stop it,*" he demanded. "There is nothing to forgive. You had an accident, and you fell. You didn't want this to happen, Branna. Come on, baby. I *know* that."

I continued to sob.

"I won't be able to live wi-with myself if I've hurt 'im—"

"*Baby,*" Ryder stressed. "Don't do this to yourself. You'll make yourself sick if you keep stressing out like this, and *that* won't be good for the baby, right?"

I took a few deep breaths.

"No," I sniffled. "It won't be g-good for the baby."

"Exactly," he stated. "We have a plan. We're going to get you warm then into clean, dry clothes. I'll pack our stuff, and we'll be on our way home in the next twenty minutes, okay?"

I nodded. "Okay."

Ryder made good on his word. After I dried and put on multiple layers of clothes, Ryder packed our belongings in record time. Things that weren't needed were abandoned in the cabin, and without giving our beautiful getaway a proper goodbye, we left, got into our Jeep, and began the journey home.

The drive down the mountain on the back roads was stomach churning. The rain was falling heavily, the thunder and lightning hadn't stopped, and the wind was so strong it caused whistling sounds to fill the car.

My cries became silent, my tears dried up, but my worries still lingered.

"I shouldn't have left the cabin," I said.

"Don't, Branna," Ryder said firmly. "Playing the what-if game will only upset you more than you already are."

He was right. I knew he was right, but my mind apparently liked torture.

"Talk about something' else," I implored. "Anythin' else."

He did just that.

We talked about anything and everything for the first two hours of our journey. I even fell asleep for a while, and when I awoke, we were back in Dublin about only twenty or so minutes away from the hospital. The weather was just as bad as it was on the mountains, but luck was on our side when it came to traffic. Smarter people than us stayed in their homes and off the roads.

"About our fight," I said to Ryder. "I'm sorry."

"No, I'm sorry," he said. "I should have never been such a dick about why I want five kids, and I should have never pushed the idea on you. It wasn't fair."

I remained silent.

"The reason I want five is just because me and my brothers make up five, and I want my kids to have what we have. I want them to have safety, security, love, and loyalty. Before you, my siblings were the only people to offer me any of that." Ryder's shoulders slumped as he spoke. "My brothers saved me growing up. Without them, I honestly don't know what kind of person I would have become back on the compound. It's just... if anything ever happens to us, I want our children to have brothers or sisters who will help and love them through anything. Apart from you and our baby, Branna, my brothers are my greatest love. They mean everything to me. I'd die for them without hesitation. I guess... I guess I just wanted the baby to have a bond like that too, and I just assumed a bond like that would be in numbers. I'm sorry for forcing my wish onto you, though. I didn't understand why you didn't want more kids, but I do now. You aren't an incubator to just house our kids. It's your decision on how many—"

"Ours," I corrected.

Ryder's eyebrow rose as he glanced for the road to me and back to the road.

"What?"

"Ours," I repeated. "I was wrong before. It's *our* decision. It *is* me body, but if I'm bein' honest, it's your body, too. You love and cherish it—you love and cherish *me*. Hearin' your reasons for why you are so adamant about wantin' five kids isn't crazy. It's heart-warmin', honey. You're such a good man, and I can't believe that you're mine. I will have as many kids as you and God give me. I want our children to have what you and I had growin' up. Love, happiness, and everything else you listed. Whether it's with one sib-lin' or ten. I want all of that... with you."

Ryder grabbed my hand for a second then let it go so he could shift gears.

"I want to kiss you so damn bad right now."

I smiled. "You'll just have to give me an extra-long one later."

"You can count on it, darling."

My heart thrummed against my chest.

"I love you, Ry," I said, my eyes misting. "You mean the world to me."

I gasped when he suddenly pulled the car over on the side of the road, unbuckled his belt, and leaned over the console to kiss me.

"There is only so much of your sweet talking I can take," he murmured against my lips. "I'm only a man."

I smiled and pressed my forehead against his before he moved back to his side of the car, buckled his belt, and started driving once more.

"You should ring your sister."

I lost my smile.

"No," I said. "I don't want to worry 'er until I know there is somethin' to worry about."

Ryder glanced at me once more.

"She'll lose her mind if you do that."

"I don't care," I said firmly. "She and everyone else will just worry, and I don't want to think about that. I just want you and me to go to the hospital, and we'll go from there, okay?"

"Whatever you want, baby."

I nodded and placed my hands on my stomach, silently willing the baby to move, but like before, I felt no movement of any kind... not even a flutter. When we pulled into the hospital car park, it wasn't soon enough. I opened the passenger door and stepped out, but the second I put weight on my sore leg, I yelped.

"Shite," I said through clenched teeth. "I can walk, but it's goin' to be sore."

Ryder came around my side of the car, shut the door, locked the car, and then scooped me up into his arms. Instinctively, my arms went around his neck as he briskly walked across the car park, through the double doors and into the hospital. I told him how to get to the emergency room, but he ignored me and the security guard, and took the stairs two at a time until we reached the second floor.

The labour ward.

"I'm not in labour," I said to him as he advanced towards the double doors. "I have to go to the emergency department."

"Like hell," he said before literally kicking the door open and stepping onto the ward.

"Ryder!" I gasped.

"Sally, Ash?" he shouted, not caring that everyone else on the ward could hear him. "I need your help; it's Branna!"

CHAPTER SEVEN

I looked to my left and saw Ash literally sprinting down the hallway with Sally and my other co-workers in tow.

"Bran," Ash panted as he came to a skidding stop before Ryder and me. "What the hell happened?"

"She fell into the river near the cabin we were staying in," Ryder answered, hiking me up against his chest so he could adjust his grip on my body. "She was submerged for about ten to fifteen seconds, and it was ice cold so I had to warm her up before we could come here. She hasn't felt the baby move since it happened nearly three hours ago."

"Room one is free," Sally said as she dug her phone from her pocket. "Get 'er in there, and I'll call me husband up from the emergency room."

Ryder kept me in his arms as he followed Ash into room one. Ryder placed me on the bed and remained by my side as Ash silently moved around the room, grabbing everything he would need to check on the baby. He cursed when he found no CTG machine in the room.

"I'll go grab a CTG," he said to Sally who entered the room.

"There is a Fetal Doppler in here. I'll use that until you get a machine. I'm sure Branna and Ryder are anxious to hear the baby's heartbeat."

If there is a heartbeat.

I began crying, and it caused Ryder to sit on the bed next to me and wrap his arm around me. Ash left the room quickly, and Sally grabbed the Fetal Doppler from the storage press at the end of the room. Ryder helped me remove my jacket and jumper and pull up my t-shirt until my belly was exposed. Sally helped me tug down my leggings until my pubic bone showed. Without waiting for consent, she squirted some gel on my stomach, turned on the Doppler, and placed it on my stomach. She swirled it around the gel, and for a few moments there was static and the usual sound that came from the device. I listened hard, and when I heard the soft drum of a heartbeat, I knew it wasn't mine from the pace of it. The sound got louder and louder until it was all that could be heard.

"The heartbeat is strong," Sally announced, and her sigh of relief was obvious. "The baby is okay, probably just sleepin'."

I burst into tears once more, and I think Ryder did too.

"I told you," he said as he kissed my face. "I told you he would be okay."

I clung to him; the relief I felt was almost too much to bear.

"Shit, don't tell me it's bad, Sal?"

I looked up and saw Ash re-enter the room, pushing a CTG machine with one hand, and pulling a USG machine behind him. The CTG machine monitors the baby's heartbeat around the clock with a strap that is placed around my stomach, whereas the USG machine is used to perform ultrasound scans.

"The opposite," Sally beamed. "The baby is fine, just sleeping."

Ash placed his hand on his chest. "Thank fuck for that."

I managed a laugh.

"I've to check on a few patients," Sally suddenly said, and she took my hand and gave it a squeeze. "Ash, get her hooked up to the CTG and I'll perform a scan in about five minutes. Ryder, join me outside for a moment, would you?"

He did so without hesitation and Ash closed the door after the pair left.

I knew Sally was giving Ryder a rundown on the procedure for this type of patient admission, and she would ask him more questions to determine if I needed to stay in the hospital overnight. I was certain I'd have to stay overnight, especially if Sally put the decision to Ryder. I turned my focus from them to my friend and snorted. Ash, as usual, had a grin on his face that told me he was about to take my mind off everything that had just happened.

"You missed me that much that you pulled this shit just so you could come onto the ward and see me?" he asked, his hand on his chest. "I'm touched."

I laughed. "Kiss me arse, I don't love you *that* much."

"Lies," he teased as he switched on the CTG machine and hooked the monitoring strap around my stomach.

I shook my head, smiling. "You should have seen Ryder run up here with me. I tried to tell 'im that this was the labour ward, and I'd need to go to the emergency department downstairs, but he wasn't havin' it."

"He trusts Sally and me to take care of you," Ash said, his chest swelling with pride. "I'd have just requested that you be brought up here anyway, so Ryder saved us time by doing this favour."

I smiled. "I figured as much."

Ash winked then looked at the USG machine that was next to us.

"I'm going to see if I can do this technician gig," he announced, rubbing his hands together before turning the machine on.

I chortled as he adjusted the CTG monitoring strap.

"Go for it," I said.

After spurting some more gel onto my skin, Ash swirled the Doppler around on my belly, and I watched him with great amusement. I didn't think he'd find the baby's heartbeat, or the baby at all, because while he was decent at reading ultrasounds, he wasn't very good at using this machine to find the perfect images. We didn't have the eye that the technicians did. To me, everything was just black and grey splotches until something was pointed out to me.

After a minute or two, I thought Ash was about to give up when he suddenly leaned in so close to the monitor that his nose almost touched the screen. He sat back on the bed after a moment and looked from the screen to me then back at the screen. He blinked and rubbed his eyes a couple of times too. I watched him with bewilderment; the man stared at the monitor like God himself had appeared and randomly began to shuffle back and forth in an Elvis costume.

"What the heck is wrong with you?" I asked with a strained laugh.

In the back of my mind, I was worried he saw something about the baby that wasn't good, and it began to scare me.

"Nothing," he replied, still looking at the screen. "I just... it looks like... I'm certain anyway—"

"Ash!" I cut him off, now panicked. "What do you see? Is the baby okay?"

Please be okay.

"Yeah, everything looks great. It's just..." he mumbled to himself and leaned in *closer* to the monitor. "Look, I'm no technician, sweetheart, but that's twins right there. I'm sure of it."

For a second, all I heard was static noise.

"I'm sorry," I said as I gathered my bearings. "Can you *repeat* that?"

"Ryder has mighty sperm," Ash stated with a shake of his head. "He knocked you up with *twins*. I'd bet my car on it."

My heart slammed into my chest because Ash bloody loved his car.

"I don't find you one bit fu-unny," I stammered. "You clearly have some other lady's ultrasound and are pretendin' it's mine!"

Laughter burst free from Ash.

"That *would* have been hilarious, but this is *not* a joke. With my hand on my heart, I'm not yanking your chain. That's all you on the screen *and* your two babies."

I looked from Ash to the screen and said, "Point it out to me."

He did as he was asked, and once I saw what he saw, I couldn't unsee it.

"Oh, my God," I whispered.

"Yep, start prayin' to Him because you're so screwed." He snickered. "Raising twins is going to be hard as hell."

Stop talking.

I thought of Ryder, and my heart began to violently pound against my chest.

"Ryder," I rasped. "Get 'im in here. Sally too; she can read scans like the newspaper."

Ash didn't need to be asked twice; he left the room and went to get Ryder and Sally. It left me alone in the room with the monitor that was now dark because the Doppler wasn't on my stomach anymore. Blank screen or not, I couldn't look away from the monitor. My whole life was changing before me, and I was sickly excited about it.

"Twins," I whispered aloud.

Can I really be that lucky?

Sally entered the room a few seconds before Ryder, and she went straight to the USG machine and repeated what Ash did. She gasped once or twice, and then took a shitload of measurements. The suspense was almost killing me.

"Well?" I said.

Sally looked at me with wide eyes. "Ash is right, Bran."

"Oh, my God!" I whispered.

"Is there something wrong with the baby?" Ryder asked, the fear in his voice evident. "Ash said something to Sally, and she just took off back in here."

I looked at my husband and found his eyes locked on mine. I shook my head in response to his question, my eyes misting with water.

"No." I choked. "In fact, *both* babies are doin' excellent."

Ryder's shoulders sagged with relief briefly before they tensed almost instantly when my words registered with him.

"Don't play," he warned. "I can't take jokes like that."

I smiled wide as tears began to splash onto my cheeks.

"I'm not playin'. We're havin' twins. Look."

Sally pointed Baby A and Baby B out to us both, and before we knew it, the whole room was crying. Even Ash was discreetly rubbing at his eyes and calling us all crybabies, which made us laugh.

"I don't know how it was missed at your twelve-week scan, Branna," Sally said, dabbing her cheeks with a hanky.

"It was a brief scan with Taylor," I said, feeling like I was floating. "And from what was pointed out to me, it did look like just one baby."

"Maybe one twin was hiding behind the other," Ash suggested. "That's happened two other times this year when the mother's had early scans."

"Will they be like my brothers?" Ryder asked me.

"No, because your brothers are *technically* fraternal twins."

Ryder blinked. "No, they're identical."

"They have different hair colour," I said flatly. "Identical twins would have the same melanin levels, so they can't have different hair colour."

My husband frowned. "Branna, apart from their hair, they are the same. They *literally* have the same face."

"I know that," I assured him. "To the world they are identical, but in medical terms, they'd be classed as fraternal twins based on their hair colour alone."

"How can they looked the exact same if they aren't identical?" he questioned, unconvinced. "They don't just look similar; they have the same everything just not the same hair."

"They are just one of nature's loopholes, I guess. They are the exact same but with different hair colour. I'm just sayin' that accordin' to science, they'd be classed as fraternal."

Ryder whistled. "Never tell them that; they think they're identical."

"I won't say a word." I chuckled as I looked at the screen then at Sally. "I'm confident *our* babies are identical, but can you confirm it?"

Sally nodded. "They're identical, honey."

"How can you tell?" Ryder questioned as he took the seat next to the bed I was lying on and grabbed my hand, squeezing it tightly.

"Fraternal twins are like any other siblings; the only difference is they share a womb. Identical twins come from the same egg thus share the same DNA pattern. There is no membrane dividin' your twins, and they're sharin' a placenta meanin' they come from the same egg that has split," Sally explained. "I've seen scans like this hundreds of times over the years, and this one is textbook for identical twins."

Ryder exhaled a deep breath. "Can you tell their gender?"

"I can." Sally hesitated as she glanced between us. "Branna is sixteen weeks and four days along, and they're both in the perfect position for gender to be determined and confirmed. Would you like to know?"

I had planned *not* to find out, but that was *before* I found out we were having bloody twins.

"I want to," I admitted to Ryder. "Do you?"

He quickly nodded, making me laugh as I looked at Sally. "We'd like to know, please, Sal."

"You're havin' identical twin boys." She beamed with a clap of her hands. "Congratulations."

"Boys," I whispered.

"It really *is* Dominic and Damien all over again," Ryder replied, his grip on my hand tightening.

"Bollocks," I spluttered.

My husband laughed. "You can say that again."

"Bollocks," I repeated, and laughed when Ryder laughed harder.

Sally and Ash left the room without us even noticing because we were so wrapped up in one another and the news we were having twins. *Identical* twins.

"Oh, God," I managed to say through the happy tears that flowed. "I'm goin' to get *huge*."

Ryder laughed and hugged me to him. "I can't believe this, Sweetness. Twin boys."

I couldn't wrap my head around it either.

"Two kids down," I said offhandedly. "Three to go."

Ryder laughed again and squeezed me so tight it almost hurt.

"I swear I will take care of all three of you," he vowed when he pulled back and stared at me. "I never thought I'd have this life."

"Me either. We've hit the jackpot."

He kissed me, and then kissed my stomach. For an hour, we talked, still in shock, but kept crying and laughing when we were overcome with happiness. Sally and Ash popped in every so often to check on me, and they even took some blood to run tests once I mentioned how laboured my breathing had been over the last few weeks along with my tiredness. Once the *babies* woke up and started moving about, my heart relaxed.

Both my and Ryder's attention was turned to the door when it opened not long after Sally went on her break.

"Dr Harris." I smiled. "Great to see you."

"Branna." He smiled warmly then shook Ryder's hand. "Ryder."

"How are you?" I asked after he gave me a hug.

"I'm great," he said, but frowned at me. "You aren't doing so hot, though."

I winced and looked at the chart in his hand.

"You got my bloodwork back already?"

Dr Harris nodded. "The lab did me a favour."

"So." I exhaled. "What's wrong with me?"

"You have anaemia, Branna. Very bad anaemia from the state of your bloodwork. Both an iron and a folate deficiency. I'm surprised you haven't come in sooner for blood tests. Haven't you been feelin' more than just a little breathless?"

Yes.

"I didn't think it was anythin' bad." I frowned. "I just thought the weather change was makin' me feel sluggish."

Ryder's hold on my hand tightened.

"Is it serious?" he asked.

Dr Harris shook his head, and I practically felt the worry leave Ryder's body.

"If left untreated, it can cause complications, but once treated, both she and the babies will be right as rain." Dr Harris looked at me. "I'm prescribin' you iron tablets *and* folic acid tablets. I know you're a midwife and all that jazz, but you're gettin' the same talkin' to as all me other patients. You *need* to take the tablets every day, and changin' your diet a bit to get more intake of the substances in food wouldn't hurt either. You and the babies will benefit greatly."

"She'll take the pills and change her diet," Ryder replied firmly. "I'll make sure of it. Don't worry, sir."

Bossy man.

I sighed. "I'll take them, even if they *are* horse-sized tablets."

Dr Harris laughed, and Ryder smirked.

"So," Dr Harris said as he glanced back at my chart, "your babies share a placenta, so you know what that means?"

It meant not only were my twins identical, but also that sharing a placenta could have problems.

I nodded. "More frequent check-ups to monitor the pregnancy closer."

"Exactly. We want this to go as smoothly as possible."

"Is her pregnancy high risk?" my husband asked.

"Higher risk than most because it's a twin pregnancy, but her anaemia is actually quite common. Things will only go in a direction we don't want if she doesn't get regular check-ups and report any problems she is havin', no matter *how* small."

Dr Harris was definitely chastising me because being a midwife, I should know better, and because he was correct, I only nodded.

He gestured to my leg. "You sure you don't want to be transferred to—"

"No," I cut him off. "It's not broken; it's just bruised. They'll want me to do an x-ray, and I won't have one being pregnant, so there is no point in goin'.'"

Dr Harris nodded in understanding. "Okay, but if the swellin' doesn't go down, you get your arse to A&E. Do you hear me?"

"I hear you." I smiled.

"You'll be stayin' overnight with us," he then stated.

I sighed but didn't protest, knowing it was for the best.

"I just want you to stay hooked up to the CTG for the night then you'll be discharged come mornin'," he added. "Just to be safe, okay?"

I nodded. "Will I be moved to the lower wards?"

"And take you away from Sally?" He snorted. "Even though you're not in labour, sweetheart, there isn't a chance I'd leave 'ere with me testicles intact if I signed off on *that*."

Ryder choked on his laughter while I embraced mine.

"It's gettin' late," Dr Harris said. "Get some sleep; it'll be sunrise before we know it."

It *was* pretty late, and at the reminder, exhaustion suddenly struck.

"I'll have a fold-up bed brought up—"

"He'll just sleep with me." I cut him off, smiling. "There isn't a point in havin' one brought up when he won't use it."

Dr Harris grinned. "I understand."

He hugged me and shook Ryder's hand before he left us alone. I was still in my clothes, and Ryder was still in his, but it didn't matter. Both of our babies were okay and healthy, and that was all that mattered. Before I drifted off into a much-needed slumber, I wondered how my sister would take the news, and without realising it, I dozed off with a huge smile on my face.

CHAPTER EIGHT

"**A**re you ready for this?"

Ryder glanced at me when I asked the question as we pulled into our driveway. It was just after nine in the morning, and I had just been discharged from the hospital. I had a headache from not sleeping well, but I was sick with excitement to share the news of our twins with our family.

"I'm ready," he said. "Are you?"

"I'm ready for a shower," I replied, "*and* some good food."

"Me too," my husband said as he glanced at the car parked next to ours, "but your sister and my brother are already here, so we'd best tackle them first."

"You shouldn't have phoned Bronagh," I said to him. "We could have just told them what happened when we got 'ere."

"*She* rang *me* to make sure we were okay after the storm last night, and she just so happened to hear Ash talking in the background," he stated as he unbuckled his seatbelt. "Not even I could talk my way out of that; your sister is too clever for her own good."

That she was.

"You could have just said we were stoppin' in on our way home from—"

"We aren't supposed to be home from the cabin for another three days," Ryder cut me off.

I opened my mouth to speak but closed it when I realised he was right.

"Are you laughin' at me?" I asked as he got out of the car.

He was clearly smiling as he rounded the car to my side and opened the door, but he said, "At you, my love? Never."

I took his hand as he helped me out of the car.

"You're full of shite," I told him.

He vibrated with silent laughter but stopped when the door to our house opened.

"Why didn't you call me?" Bronagh shouted.

Here we go.

"I didn't want you to worry—offt."

I was cut off as my little sister charged at me, only slowing her pace briefly before she reached me to wrap her arms around me as she gave me a bone-crushing hug.

"Jesus, Bronagh." Ryder scowled. "Be careful with her."

"She's pregnant, not made of glass," my sister said to him before she looked down at my leg and realised it was bent.

"What happened?" she asked, her brows furrowed.

I sighed. "It's a story that should only be told over a cuppa."

"Dominic," Bronagh shouted. "Put on the kettle."

"I already did," came his voice from the doorway.

I looked around my sister and saw Dominic standing on the top step with my niece in his arms.

"Georgie!" I squealed.

I halted when Ryder's hand gripped my forearm.

"What?"

He frowned. "I'll carry you."

"You'll make a show of me," I informed him.

He rolled his eyes. "Everyone is still in bed—"

"Morning, neighbours!"

Ryder closed his eyes. "Except for Alec."

I turned and waved at my brother-in-law who was getting his mail from the post box next to his front door in just his boxer shorts.

It was so typically Alec being Alec that I didn't even flinch.

"It's a cold one," I shouted. "Huh?"

He looked down to his groin then back up at me and said, "You're a smartass."

We all laughed.

"Come over with Keela," I called out. "We have to tell you guys somethin'."

"We'll be over in ten," he said before retreating into his house.

I barely turned back in the direction of my own house before I was lifted off the ground. I yelped and latched onto my husband, hoping I dug my nails into him a little harder than he'd like.

"You're goin' to annoy me to death," I told him.

"Safety first," was all he said.

I shook my head as he carried me inside our house with my sister hot on our heels. We gathered around the kitchen table, and when I realised one twin was missing I said, "Where's Dame?"

"Sleeping," Dominic replied like it was obvious. "We used our key, and when I looked in his room, he was snoring, so I didn't wake him."

Ryder yawned. "Go wake him now."

"Is it bad news?" my sister asked, taking the seat next to me.

I turned to her and saw fear in her eyes.

"No, baby, it's not."

"You want Alec and Keela to come over, and Damien to come downstairs," she said, unconvinced. "Somethin' is goin' on."

"It's not bad news," I assured her.

She gave me a once-over.

"I'd have been there in a second," she said and leaned into me, hugging me tightly.

"I know," I said, returning the hug, "but I didn't want to worry you."

"Worry me next time," she stated as we pulled apart. "It freaks me out knowin' you were in the hospital and I had no idea."

I didn't plan on there being a next time, but to appease her, I relented and agreed.

"I know it's early, but how is Aideen?" I asked, noting she, Kane, and Jax weren't there.

"On 'er way," Bronagh said. "We debated callin' 'er because of 'er just havin' the baby, but she wouldn't hear of it. She threatened us a time or two on the phone for even hesitatin'."

I smiled. "You would have opened a can of worms if you didn't call 'er."

"Tell us about it." Keela snorted as she strolled into the kitchen followed by a now fully dressed Alec. "She's only just calmed down from havin' Locke. There is no way in hell I wanted to piss 'er off."

After we had hugged one another, we spent the next few minutes looking at pictures of the newest addition to our family, and it only added to my excitement about Ryder's and my baby news.

"I recorded some of the labour for you," Keela said and handed me her phone.

I winced through some of the footage when I saw my friend in pain, but then I straight-up cackled at other clips.

"If you ever *approach me for sex again, I'm cuttin' your dick clean off," Aideen bellowed at Kane, who was just staring at her and rapidly blinking.*

"Babydoll, do you want—"

"What I want is for you to jump out that window right there," Aideen cut Kane off. "You did this to me!"

Ash looked at Kane. "Isn't this her second child?"

"Yeah," Kane replied.

"Then why—"

"I'm sorry," Aideen cut Ash off. "Does havin' a baby make it stop hurtin' like fuckin' hell the second time or somethin'?"

Ash bit down on his lower lip, clearly trying to hide his smile.

"No, ma'am," he replied to Aideen. "It's just as bad as the first time... or so I've been told."

Aideen leaned back into her pillow and said, "I'm surrounded by fuckin' eejits."

"Breath, Ado," Keela's voice sounded. *"You're doin' brilliant, babe."*

"Keela, I'll make you eat that fuckin' phone if you're recordin' me!" Aideen warned.

The screen went black seconds later, making me laugh.

"She was sweet as pie after she had the baby," Keela said, laughing too. "I felt sorry for everyone in the room with 'er when she was pushin' because for the few minutes I was there, she was a nightmare."

"Bran!"

I looked up at my name being shouted and smiled at a groggy Damien, who was rubbing the sleep from his eyes.

"Heya, son." I winked.

Everyone often teased us because since Damien moved back into the house, I had become somewhat of a mother hen to him, and he had zero objections to it.

"You look great," he beamed as he crossed the room and bent down, hugging me. "Your bump is so much bigger."

"You aren't supposed to *say* that," Dominic stated from behind his brother. "It upset Bronagh whenever you said it to her."

Damien straightened. "Bronagh's emotions were—"

"Were what?" my sister cut him off.

"All over the place," Damien finished, mischief glinting in his eyes. "You were a crying machine."

Bronagh grinned as she took Georgie from Dominic and shrugged her shoulders at Damien, not denying she was a hormonal mess whilst pregnant.

"Why were you in the hospital?" Damien asked, concern in his gaze. "Dominic mentioned it's why you're home early from your honeymoon."

"Aideen, Kane, and Alannah aren't 'ere," I said.

"We'll tell them later," my sister almost exploded with apprehension. "Please, Branna, is the baby truly okay?"

I looked at Ryder who nodded. I looked from my friends to my sister, and each of them looked scared to death, so I knew I couldn't leave them in suspense.

"Long story short, I had fallen up at the cabin, and to be safe, we went to the hospital," I explained then smiled. "It turns out that *both* of our babies are doin' really good."

Bronagh almost let Georgie fall, and if it wasn't for Dominic grabbing her, my niece would have hit the floor in seconds.

"Shut up!" my sister screeched and lunged at me. "Shut up. Shut up. *Shut up*!"

I laughed and so did Ryder.

"Both," Alec said looking at Damien. "Did she just say *both*?"

He blinked. "I think she did, brother."

"Well, fuck me sideways," Alec said. "*Another* set of twins in the family?"

I nodded, smiling.

"*Yes*!" Dominic and Damien said in unison and fist bumped one another.

"Why're you both so excited?" Ryder asked his brothers, his brows raised.

"Because," Damien grinned, "For *years,* you always said if you had twins like us, you'd know it was some form of punishment from God."

I looked at Ryder while he glared at a laughing Damien and a grinning Dominic.

"Is that true?" I asked, chuckling.

"Maybe," my husband replied, still glaring at his younger brothers.

"They're identical twin boys like you both, too," I commented.

They never needed to know that they were technically fraternal twins. No one would believe them anyway if they said they weren't identical; they look like the exact same person just with different hair colour.

The twins fist bumped again.

"Oh, man," Dominic laughed, "I'm so happy it's not me."

"Or me," Damien and Alec said in unison, making *me* laugh.

"*Identical twin boys,* Branna!"

I looked at my sister when she spoke and wrapped her arms around me once more. I heard her voice break, and it instantly brought tears to my eyes.

"I know, Bee," I said as I hugged her. "I can't believe it."

"Everyone has boys but me!" she cried, making me chuckle.

"Let's get to babymaking, and I'll put a boy in you this time... promise," Dominic chimed in.

Alec snorted. "I bet I'll have a son before you do."

Dominic punched Alec, who punched him back. Ryder had to step between them and shove them apart, which brought a big smile to my face.

Some things will never change.

I hugged everyone in the room and showed them the scan pictures of the babies.

"It's not fair that you get two out of this pregnancy and I've to go through it four more times to get the number of kids we want," Bronagh said, sliding her fingertips over the pictures in awe.

Keela snickered. "Maybe you'll have twins eventually."

Dominic placed his hand on his chest and said, "Don't you wish that upon us, Daley."

I beamed. "What's so bad about havin' twins?"

"*I'm* a twin," Dominic said, stating the obvious. "I know how much of a handful we can be."

"He speaks the truth," Damien said in agreement. "We were little shits."

"Nothing's changed," Alec mused. "You're *still* little shits."

I excused myself to use the bathroom once the twins starting rowing with Alec over how much of a little shit *he* was and is. I took my time relieving myself and cleaning up a bit before I thought of going back downstairs. I changed clothes in my room, brushed out my hair, and plaited it to keep it out of my face. When I felt a little more human, I went back downstairs but halted in the hallway when

I heard voices coming from the street.

I exited my house and walked down the steps and to the end of my garden when I spotted Alec at our gate holding a white football in his hands with three boys surrounding him.

"What's goin' on?"

Alec looked at me. "They kicked their ball at the house; I caught it when I was leaving."

"We didn't do it on purpose, missus," one of the boys almost shouted at me, pleading their case.

I recognised the boy; he was my neighbour and from a few doors down.

"You'd better not have, or I'll pop your stupid soccer ball," Alec warned them.

"Fuck you, mister," the boy snapped. "I'll tell me ma if you do."

"Kid," Alec laughed, "don't threaten me. I'll start making promises if you do."

Uh-oh.

"Yeah?" the boy snapped. "Like what? You stupid yank."

"Don't mess with me, kid," Alec warned.

"Or what?' the kid countered.

"I'll fuck your sister *and* mom then marry them both and become your step-dad and brother-in-law if you cross me again, you little shit."

The kid's face went the colour of beetroot when his friends cracked up laughing.

"Me da will kick your arse for sayin' that!" he angrily hissed at Alec.

"Then I'll fuck *his* ass and marry him too. Don't try me on this, Bilbo. I'll wifey up your entire household, and we'll all be one big happy fucking family."

The kid's face turned a darker shade of red as his friends' laughter rose.

"I'm tellin' your missus!" he spluttered.

"You almost hit my face with the ball, and she *loves* my face, so please," Alec said, and gestured towards my house where Keela was, "go ahead,"

The kid hesitated, so Alec continued, "She'll double team your brothers in front of you if you give her attitude."

The kid widened his eyes and said, "Your whole family is bloody crazy!" Then he turned and ran off, his friends following closely behind. All three of them forgot their football.

"And don't you forget it!" Alec shouted after him before kicking the ball after them. He shook his head and looked at me. "Fucking pussy looked like he was about to cry."

I had to cross my legs as laughter spilled from me accompanied by a painful stitch in my side.

"Branna?" I heard Ryder's voice call from behind me.

"She's fine," Alec shouted as he grabbed me, so I didn't fall over. "She's just laughing and possibly pissing herself."

I smacked at him with my hands as I wheezed with laughter, and he found this amusing but just for a moment.

"Shit, Bran," Alec said, panicked. "Are you okay?"

I wanted to say yes, but I couldn't because a stitch was paining me.

"Ryder!" he shouted.

"I'm fine," I rasped and placed my hands on my hips. "Just lost my breath."

"Bran?" Ryder said, his hands gripping my shoulders.

"I'm fine," I assured him. "Just laughed too hard and lost my breath."

"I'm getting your prescription from the pharmacy as soon as I get you up to bed," he stated.

I smiled when I looked up at him. "Okay, *Daddy*."

He grinned, and we looked at Alec when he grunted.

"What?" I asked.

"Nothing, I *love* witnessing sexual tension when I haven't gotten any in two days."

"Two days?" I said dryly. "How tragic."

"Tell me about it," he grunted. "Damn periods fuck my life up. I'm thankful for my hand."

Ryder laughed.

"That's what you're thankful for?" I asked Alec. "Your hand?"

"I'm thankful there are so many different ways to eat potatoes," he instantly replied.

I smiled at the thought of food.

"Me too, and for pizza. All the different styles of pizza."

Alec bumped his fist with mine.

"You're my spirit animal," he said.

I laughed. "And you're mine."

Alec went on his way to his house, and just as I turned to head back up to my house with Ryder, I spotted Kane's car driving down the road. Ryder noticed them too.

"You ready to tell them the baby news?" he asked.

I beamed. "Born ready."

"We'll get Lana later and tell her," he said. "Then that's everyone we love who knows we're having twins."

I was tired, hungry, and desperate to sleep in my own bed, but nothing could compare to the happiness I felt when Ryder's words sunk in. It was real; we were having twin boys, and everyone was happy. What felt most important to me was that *I* was happy, truly happy, and I'd be damned if it didn't feel good.

CHAPTER NINE

Twenty weeks later...

Being almost thirty-seven weeks pregnant with twins was absolute misery. Everywhere ached, everywhere was swollen, and I hadn't seen my feet in so long I was desperate to be reacquainted with the visual of my toes. I groaned then followed up with a sigh.

"They'll be here soon, Bran."

I rolled my eyes at my sister's comment. "It's easy for you to say. You're not the beached whale who can barely move without needin' help."

"I was in your shoes before." Bronagh smiled. "I know how miserable you're feelin'."

"Times that misery by two and you'll get how I'm feelin'," I grumbled.

Bronagh was silent for a moment then said, "Do you want a back or foot rub?"

"No," I said. "I'll only get sleepy but won't be able to fall asleep."

"What do you want to do then?" she asked.

I heaved myself up from my sitting position.

"I'm goin' to have a cuppa."

I left my newly furnished sitting room—Ryder decided it was time we had an actual sitting room and moved the gym upstairs—and headed into the kitchen. I smiled at Alannah, who was sitting at the kitchen table, tapping on the screen of her phone. She excused herself from the sitting room minutes ago to take a call.

"Is everything okay?" I asked as I made myself tea and headed over to the kitchen table.

"Yep, just confirmin' work stuff."

I nodded as I took the seat across from her, but the second I sat down, I tensed up when I saw the cup Alannah now had in her grasp.

"Alannah," I said with wide eyes. "That's Alec's favourite cup."

It was a silly cup that revealed a quote about being up to no good from the *Harry Potter* books when a hot liquid was poured inside. Alec loved the damn thing.

"He can use another one." She yawned then took a sip of tea. "God 'imself couldn't take this cup of tea away from me right now; it's needed."

"No, seriously," I pressed. "He has some sort of weird claim on it."

"It'll be fine." She chuckled. "It's not like he is goin' to—"

"Are you using my cup?"

I looked to my right and began laughing when I saw Alec standing at the kitchen doorway.

"For God's sake," Alannah groaned. "Did we just unknowingly summon you or somethin'?"

His gaze hardened.

"Ryan," he bit out. "Is. That. My. Cup?"

Alannah innocently smiled. "Could be, could not be."

"You're going to answer the damn question before I lose my freaking mind."

The glare Alec shot Alannah caused me to smother a smile behind my own cup of tea.

"Yep," she replied, smacking her lips together. "I am."

"That's *my* cup," Alec said through gritted teeth. "Nobody uses my cup."

"Until today, Sheldon Cooper."

Alec set his jaw when Alannah tipped the cup in his direction.

"You're being difficult," he said, his frustration not going amiss. "You're never difficult. What is wrong with you?"

Alannah shrugged. "I don't feel like being a pushover today."

"I'm *about* to push you over if you don't give me back my cup."

"What if I let the cup fall when you push me?" she asked, a brow raised.

"I've never hit a female, Alannah, but keep talking about breaking my cup and that will change. Your ass will be set aflame, woman."

Alannah stuck out her tongue, placed it on the rim of the cup, and with her eyes locked on Alec's, she slid it around the rim. When she was finished, she held the cootie-infected cup out to Alec, but he didn't move a muscle.

"You evil... bitch."

Alannah devilishly smiled. "Does this mean I can finish me tea in peace?"

Alec narrowed his eyes to slits. "You have won the battle, Ryan, but you will *not* win the war."

He turned and left the room, his weird threat lingering like a bad smell.

I looked at Alannah and said, "You know Keela is goin' to kill you for the impendin' headache you've just set up for 'er, right?"

"It was so worth it." Alannah snickered. "Did you see his face?"

I laughed. "I thought he was goin' to bite a chunk out of you. He loves that damn cup."

"I can understand why," she mused. "My hands fit around it just right."

"You're a weirdo," I teased. "You know that, right?"

"Since the day I started school." She nodded.

I smiled, sipping my own tea.

"How are you feelin'?" she asked me. "I still can't believe

you're carryin' *twins*."

"I know." I exhaled a deep breath. "It's so excitin' but honestly? I just want them to get *out*."

Alannah nodded in understanding.

"Twin identical boys, though," she continued. "You're goin' to have a bunch of daddies and brothers knockin' at your door in the future if they're anythin' like Dominic and Damien and how they were with girls."

I blessed myself.

"Don't even *mention* anythin' like that," I said to her. "I'd smack their arses red raw."

Alannah laughed. "I believe you."

I eyed her. "How are *you*?"

"Me?" She forced a smile. "I'm great."

I took a few seconds to really look at her. Alannah was a very attractive woman that I knew would be the envy of many women who saw her in passing. Her skin was porcelain pale, and while it was clear of imperfections, she had the cutest splash of freckles sprinkled over her nose and under her eyes. She rarely wore makeup, and unless you were up close and personal with her, you would think otherwise when looking at her striking face. Her cheekbones were high, her jawline defined, her eyes were large and encased by long lashes and guarded by thick, nicely shaped brows. Her eyes were soft brown, and they reminded me of an anime character. Her hair was dark as the night and flowed in waves to the base of her spine.

She was perfect, and I knew she had no idea just how beautiful she was. Usually, if someone was gorgeous, they knew it, or had some sort of hint to it, but not Alannah.

"You're a bad liar, friend," I said with a sad smile.

She dropped her forced smile. "And 'ere I thought I was a convincin' fibber."

I winked. "Not on your life."

Alannah sighed, her shoulders slumping. "I'm debatin' on whether to tell me ma about me da's affair... for real this time."

I gasped at the admission. "Really?"

She reluctantly nodded. "He knows somethin' is up with me because I refuse to be alone with 'im."

I frowned. "I can't imagine how you're feelin'."

"It hurts," Alannah said, her eyes distant. "I'm angry, sad, disappointed, and baffled. Me ma is beautiful, Branna. I'm not bein' biased either; she is really pretty, and she can cook and sing and put a smile on anyone's face without tryin'. You've met 'er so you know. She loves me da to death, which is why this is killin' me. If I don't tell 'er, me da will continue havin' the affair. She deserves a hell of a lot better than that, but if I tell her, I'll break 'er heart and ruin our family."

I covered Alannah's hand with my own.

"If anyone is to take blame for this, it's your father. Not you, not your mother, *him* and *him alone*."

Alannah nodded, but it didn't look like she believed me, and I hated that. No matter what the outcome would be for her family, she would feel somewhat to blame no matter what anyone said. That was the kind of person she was. She wanted to fix everything, and when she couldn't, she took on the weight of failure on her own two shoulders and carried it.

"I'm the only one out of our group who has both of 'er parents," she commented softly. "For ages, I thought it was because we were normal, but now... now I don't know what to think."

"We're all 'ere for you," I told her. "Please, don't bear this burden alone."

"It's hard not to. Every time I pluck up the courage to confront me da or tell me ma, I chicken out."

"I would too," I assured her. "This is heavy stuff; you have to do it only when the time is right."

Alannah nodded and retreated into the comfort of her own mind where she could think. We spoke no further on the subject when Damien walked into the room holding Georgie or when Dominic and Bronagh came in a few seconds behind them. I knew Bronagh was in the house, but the twins were supposed to be at work. Dominic got the full-time gym job at the new leisure centre in town that Ryder told me about on our honeymoon, and both Damien and Ryder got jobs at Aideen's father's auto shop as roadside rescue. They had a basic understanding of engines, but Aideen's father schooled them for weeks to expand their knowledge and make their jobs a hell of a lot easier.

"How come you're both home from work?" I quizzed.

"Lunch," the twins replied in unison.

"It's lunchtime already?" I frowned. "Dame, where is Ryd—"

"He literally just walked in the door," Bronagh cut me off as she glanced out of the kitchen towards the front door. "Damien came in ahead of 'im 'cause he was parkin' the truck."

Ryder and Damien shared the company vehicle, but Ryder did the majority of the driving.

"I forgot to make lunch," I sniffled, feeling like a horrible person.

"No tears," my sister quickly said. "I made them food while you were restin'. It's in the fridge."

"Thanks." I smiled as I rubbed at my eyes.

It didn't take much for me to cry, and when I got going, it was hard to stop.

"Dadadadada!" Georgie said as she snuggled into Damien's chest.

Dominic almost glared at his daughter. "*I'm* your dada. Damien is your *uncle*."

Bronagh rolled her eyes. "She *knows* your 'er da, but she calls *everyone* dada. It's all she can say. Also, she's a baby, and it's probably freaky figurin' out why another man has the same face as 'er daddy. She'll make that mistake until she realises who is who."

"How come *you* didn't make a mistake and find your way to my bed?" Damien asked Bronagh, grinning.

"Simple." She grinned back. "You moved away, and I got to know 'im better."

Damien's face dropped. "I *knew* I should have stayed here."

Bronagh laughed, but Dominic was less than amused.

"Give Georgie back to Bronagh," he ordered.

Damien frowned. "Why?"

"So I can kill you," came his brother's response.

Damien held onto Georgie for dear life, which I found amusing. I shook my head as I took a sip of tea. I looked back at Alannah, found her looking at Damien before she looked down at Alec's cup and swallowed. If I didn't know any better, I'd say she looked guilty of something.

Interesting.

The room became crowded when Ryder walked in, taking the seat next to me. I wasn't surprised when Alec re-entered the room with Keela minutes later and glared at Alannah as if she had just killed his parents. I snorted at him and opened a jar of mayonnaise that was on the table and grabbed some bread and ham from the fridge so I could make a sandwich. Bronagh, who was next to me, pulled a face when she smelled the jar of mayonnaise that I had opened. I watched as she covered her mouth as if the stench of it was making her feel sick. I widened my eyes at this because the only time Bronagh couldn't stand the smell of mayonnaise was when she was pregnant with Georgie.

"No. Fuckin'. Way," she said before darting out of the room and sprinting up the stairs.

I looked at Dominic who looked from the doorway to me.

I blinked. "Did you see that?"

He nodded. "You thinking what I'm thinking?"

"I think I am, but we'll have to wait and see."

"What are you two talkin' about?" Keela asked from the kitchen table.

"You'll see," I said, earning a snicker from Dominic.

"No. Fuckin'. Way!" my sister repeated from the upstairs bathroom five minutes later then ran back down the stairs

I looked at Dominic, and we both smiled as she slid into the kitchen.

She was *so* pregnant.

Bronagh was pale white. Dominic smiled, I smiled, Ryder clicked his tongue, and the rest of the group stared at us with raised brows.

"Why're you both smiling?" Damien asked Dominic and me.

"Because," he beamed and flung his arm around Bronagh when she moved to his side holding a white stick, "I'm going to be a daddy again."

Everyone gasped, and that was when Bronagh spoke.

"You have a magical dick," she said to Dominic and hugged him tightly.

"I *told* you that," he stressed as he hugged her back.

"I bet it's a boy," Alec said off hand.

"Georgie's gonna have her hands full with males, if that's the case," Ryder mumbled aloud. "That'd make five boys including the twins, right? Aideen's not pregnant again... or is she?"

We all laughed at the jest.

"Let's make a list," Alec suggested, and held up his hand to count the children. "Aideen and Kane have two boys, Dominic and Bronagh have one girl and one on the way, Ry and Branna are having twin boys, Keela and I are having one—that we know of—and that's it so fa—"

"What?" I cut Alec off and spun around to Keela who was smiling wide.

"You're *pregnant*?" I asked on a gasp.

She nodded. "I found out yesterday, and we went to the doctor's this mornin'. I'm seven weeks along based on when I got me last period. It could be a little less, but I'm definitely one hundred percent up the duff."

I screamed, Alannah screamed, Bronagh screamed, Keela screamed, and Georgie screamed.

"Is there anyone else who *isn't* pregnant?" Damien asked throwing his hands up in the air. "Because this is getting out of hand.

Brothers, keep your dicks in your damn pants. Overpopulation is a *serious* global problem and you four are adding to it big time!"

The brothers laughed at Damien then they each clapped Dominic and Alec on the back, congratulating them while us girls jumped around with high-pitched voices and a lot of oh my Gods being spoken. It was during the commotion that we didn't hear Kane, Aideen, and the boys enter the house.

"Why're you all so happy?" Aideen shouted over us, getting our attention.

She pointed at me. "Don't be jumpin' around when you're so close to birthin' twins."

I rooted myself to the spot. "She's right; jumpin' around isn't exactly encouraged by pregnant women. With more than one of us being pregnant too, we'd better quit it."

"Who else is pregnant besides Branna?" Aideen asked, an eyebrow raised.

She almost instantly began screaming when Bronagh and Keela raised their hands. She pretty much tackled them both with a hug before doing the same to Dominic and Alec, who laughed at her and returned her hug happily.

"I'm so glad it's not me," Aideen said, making us all laugh.

Kane snorted. "You'll probably be pregnant again before they give birth, and you know it."

Aideen whirled on him and dangerously pointed a finger at his face.

"We already decided on a *two-year* break before we start tryin' again," she reminded him. "We have to enjoy Jax and Locke before we have more kids. That was the agreement."

Kane, who was holding his sons, took a step backwards.

"I remember, Babydoll. I'm just saying, you got pregnant both times when—"

"You aren't goin' raw for two years, Germinator, so accept it already."

Kane scowled at Aideen's dismissal of their conversation while his brothers offered him apologetic pats on the back as if having to wear a condom during sex was a prison sentence.

"How *are* me stunnin' nephews?" I asked, switching the topic of discussion to the boys.

Kane handed a sleeping Locke to me while Damien took Jax and Georgie to the far side of the room where their toy chest was. I nestled Locke against my chest as best as I could, but with my belly being so huge and him being big himself, it made the task a difficult one. Ryder took pity on my struggle and took the baby from me, settling his sleeping form against his broad shoulder.

I sighed. "I can't wait to not be pregnant."

"How long till you're induced?" Aideen quizzed.

"Four more days if I don't go into labour myself before then," I said, my shoulders slumping. "They're both expected to be six pounders, which is big for twins. Dr Harris wants them out before they get any bigger since I'm plannin' a vaginal birth—trustin' nothin' goes unexpectedly wrong."

"We can go walkin' again later and get us some spicy foods," Aideen offered. "Hopefully, it will kick-start things into action."

"I'll try anythin' but sex at this point because it hurts so feckin' bad."

Aideen winced. "Sex never hurt me."

"Thank God," Kane said from across the room where he and Alec were looking at something on their phones.

Ryder snorted in response but didn't speak—probably in fear he'd wake Locke.

"I wish I could stay longer," Alannah announced, "but I've to go and interview someone who applied for me assistant job."

Alannah's graphic and design business was taking on a life of its own. She was growing an impressive clientele list, and with the joy of a booming business came chaos. She needed someone to help manage some of it, so she could focus on her job of creating something that fit with the vision of each client.

"How are you goin' to get there?" Aideen quizzed. "I know

your car is at me da's garage gettin' a diesel pump repaired."

"I was goin' to walk." Alannah shrugged.

"I can drop you," Damien offered, straightening up from playing with the kids. "Ry and I don't need to be back in work for an hour and thirty minutes."

Alannah was hesitant. "I don't want to be a bother."

"You're never a bother." Damien said, his cheeks flaring with a little bit of heat. "We can get lunch or something after your inter-view if you aren't busy. "

"I can't." She swallowed.

"Why not?" Damien asked, crossing the room, frowning.

Alannah avoided looking in Aideen's direction, which I found weird.

"I'm kind of seein' someone," she said in a whisper.

Everyone went deathly silent, even the kids; it was like they knew something was up.

"Who?" Bronagh asked first.

"Yeah," Damien said, his voice shockingly low. "Who?"

"It doesn't matter who—"

"It bloody well does!" Bronagh cut Alannah off.

Alannah looked at her friend. "I was goin' to tell you, I promise, but I knew you'd tell Aideen, and I didn't want a big deal to be made out of it."

"Why would she tell me?" Aideen quizzed with furrowed brows. "And why would a big deal be made out of it?"

Alannah groaned and put her face in her hands.

"Oh, my God," Bronagh suddenly gasped. "It's one of 'er broth-ers, isn't it?"

"What?" Aideen asked, her eyes wide. "You're goin' out with one of me brothers?"

Alannah looked up, and instead of looking at Aideen, she looked at Damien as she said, "Yes."

Damien balled his hands into fists. "Which Collins?"

I leaned against Ryder's shoulder as she said, "Dante."

Oh, shite.

"I've got to go," Damien said and made a move to walk out of the room.

Alannah grabbed his arm. "Wait. Look, we need to talk."

"No," Damien said and removed her hand from his arm. "We don't."

"Please, I don't know why I've brought this up, but we have to try—"

"I *have* tried with you." He angrily cut her off. "I've tried to be patient. I've tried to show you how sorry I am for what I did to you. I've tried to befriend you. I've tried to give you space... I've tried to show you how much I care about you, but you don't want me. I see that now."

"Damien—"

"No, Alannah," he cut her off. "You're with Dante Collins, and I'm done."

"It's not a relationship," she blurted. "We aren't datin'. He is just... there."

"What the hell does *that* mean?" Aideen angrily snapped.

Alannah didn't look away from Damien's back.

"He helped me get over you—"

"By getting under *him*?" he snapped.

Alannah winced. "That's not fair, Damien. You were gone for so long, and we weren't on good terms."

"I left *for* you!" Damien shouted as he spun around to face Alannah. "When I realised how much I hurt you, when Bronagh told me the things no one else would, I made the decision to leave to better myself but also to give you time. I didn't know how to attempt to make things right back then, but I was always going to come back for you, Alannah. I was going to fix everything, but you've made it so hard."

Alannah's voice cracked. "I... I didn't know."

Damien shook his head. "I have to go."

He turned around and walked out of the kitchen, but Alannah

quickly followed him while we all stayed rooted to the spot.

"Damien, please," she pleaded from the hallway.

Georgie began to cry, which prompted Jax to become distressed also.

"Let go, Lana," he replied, his tone low.

She has hold of him.

"No," she shouted. "We need to talk."

"What we need to do is be away from each other," Damien replied. "Go to Dante; I'm sure he'll be more than happy to comfort you."

"Damien, stop. You don't mean that."

"Alannah. Let. Go."

"No, I won't."

My eyes slid to Bronagh after she got Georgie from the play area. She tried to hand her daughter to Dominic, but he only hooked an arm around Bronagh's waist, keeping both of his girls in place.

"Let them figure this out *themselves*," he said into her ear.

"Does it *sound* like they're figurin' anythin' out?" she quipped while bouncing Georgie to calm her.

Aideen took out her phone and began tapping on the screen. Kane, who was looking over her shoulder as he consoled Jax, groaned and looked up at the ceiling when she sent whatever message she texted.

"This is going to be bad," he murmured to Ryder and Alec.

They nodded in unison.

"Why do you want to talk all of a sudden?" Damien demanded from the hallway. "Why not the first million times I asked?"

"Because I'm ready to deal with all of this."

"It took you long enough!"

"Don't be nasty," Alannah hit back. "None of this is me fault. *I'm* the one who was hurt and embarrassed and have been carryin' it around for years, not you."

"Not me?" Damien bellowed. "I've carried it around since the second I did you wrong, and I fucking know it. I *know* what I did, and I've tried to make it right, but I can't. You've made it impossible."

"How?" Alannah asked.

"By being with *him*!" Damien roared. "I haven't touched anyone since I touched you. I haven't kissed anyone since I kissed you. I haven't looked at another woman since I was fucking eighteen, but that ends tonight. If you have moved on, then so will I."

I felt my mouth drop open with shock at Damien's admission, and so did everyone else's.

"Fine," Alannah screamed, but I heard it in her voice that she was going to cry. "Go be with some bitch 'cause I won't be here when you get back. You say you're done? Well, so am I!"

Damien humourlessly laughed. "You've been done with me for years, and you know it!"

I jumped when the hall door opened and slammed shut. Bronagh handed over Georgie then pushed away from Dominic and ran out to the hallway when Alannah's crying could be heard. I turned and gripped Ryder's arm after he handed Locke back to his mother.

"Go after 'im," I pleaded with my husband. "He will never forgive 'imself if he gets with someone tonight. He loves 'er, Ryder, and she loves 'im. They just need to figure a lot of shite out before they get to the point where they both realise it."

Ryder nodded and looked at his brothers.

"It'll take *all* of us to talk some sense into him," he said.

My heart hurt. Everything in my personal life with Ryder was perfect, but Alannah and Damien were a part of my life overall, and I couldn't stand by while they both self-destructed.

"We have to help them," I said to the girls.

I could hear Bronagh trying to comfort Alannah, but I heard that she was semi-crying too. It hurt her when Alannah hurt, just like it was hurting the other girls and me to see her in this state.

"What will we do?" Aideen asked while the brothers muttered to one another.

"If she isn't serious about 'im, then she needs to end whatever she has goin' on with Dante," Keela said. "I know it sounds awful, but that's what needs to be done if she wants a chance with Damien."

We nodded in agreement.

Keela looked at Aideen. "Your brothers are only comin' around to Kane's brothers now, but that progress will halt if Damien jumps Dante out of hurt and anger. None of your brothers will stand by and let that happen. If Dante gets the better of Damien, Dominic will step in, and then Harley will be on 'im like a bad rash, and Kane will get involved and so on. It will cause nothin' but trouble."

Aideen sighed. "I know. I've messaged Dante, the stupid fuck
—"

She cut herself off when her phone began to ring.

"Speak of the devil," she muttered before she answered her phone and put it to her ear. "You're a stupid bastard ruled by his dick, do you know that?" she snapped.

The lads stopped talking and focused on Aideen and her conversation with her brother.

"Do you realise the shit storm you're involved in?" She continued talking over her brother, who was trying to get a word in but couldn't. "Damien and Alannah just had a big argument, and she revealed she is sleepin' with *you*, you nasty fuck. They both have a thing for one another and have for years but are *horrible* at being honest and talkin' about their feelins'. Alannah is in tears 'ere, and Damien will probably have a go at you if he comes across you."

Aideen paused, then shouted, "I don't bloody know where he is. He's on his lunch break so he's probably gone to some pub to drink it out. Why?"

She gasped after Dante replied to her question.

"Don't you *dare* go and look for 'im, do you hear me? You can't fix this. What's done is done—Hello? *Hello?*"

Aideen pulled the phone away from her ear and looked at it.

"That bastard just hung up on me."

"I'm sure he lost service," Kane said while rubbing his right temple.

"He didn't lose service; he hung up on me."

If there was one person in the world who you didn't hang up on, it was Aideen Collins.

"Forget that," I stated. "Did he say he was goin' to *look* for Dame?"

"Yeah," Aideen said with a shake of her head. "He thinks he can explain everythin' to 'im. He'll probably wait until Damien's lunch break is over, and I don't want this confrontation to happen at the shop. Dante, the fuckin' eejit will talk about his and Lana's sex life, and Damien will try to kill 'im. Oh God, Kane!"

Aideen spun to her one and only, and he instantly invaded her space, kissed her forehead and said, "We're on it."

Kane, Alec, and Ryder left the kitchen, while Dominic lingered by my sister when she re-entered the room without Alannah.

"She's gone home and wouldn't let me go with 'er. She's already a mess about 'er da's affair, and how to handle that, but this will rip 'er apart unless we help fix this."

"This is so bad," Keela said.

"Go with your brothers to talk Damien down," Bronagh said to Dominic as she wiped her puffy red eyes and took Georgie from him. "You know how he feels about Alannah. We have to stop this before he goes too far."

He hesitated. "Are you sure?"

"Don't worry about me. It's been weeks since Georgie weaned. I miss the closeness I had with 'er when she nursed, but I'm good now. You've helped me through this, and Branna and the girls have me back when you aren't 'ere. We're goin' to be parents again too. I'm better than I've ever been."

Dominic exhaled a deep breath. "Thank God. I knew you were going through a tough time, and I tried my best to be patient with you, but hell, you were such an asshole these past few weeks."

"Did you just call me an arsehole?" Bronagh said, her attention focused completely on her fiancé.

"Hell no," he quickly replied when he realised his slipup. "I said your ass is *goals*."

Bronagh's lips twitched. "Nice save, *dickhead*."

He teasingly grinned. "You'll give my dick head? Fantastic!"

He reached for Bronagh, but she jumped away from him, giggling. Georgie squealed with delight and clapped her hands together.

"Go help your brother!" She nudged him. "We'll get to work on how we can help things on Alannah's end."

I looked at the pair and shook my head, smiling from ear to ear. Dominic got a few kisses out of Bronagh and an arse grab, of course, and cuddles from his daughter before he left with his brothers to seek out Damien and get knee-deep into his problems. Many new things were happening to our group—some big changes and some little ones—but it was nice to see that at least some things never changed. No matter what any one of us went through, I knew I could always count on us pulling together to help one another out. We weren't just friends; we were more than that.

We were family, and we'd go to the ends of the Earth for one another.

Here is a Sneak Peek at the First Chapter of

DAMIEN

Releasing in 2017

PROLOGUE

Five and a half years ago…

*B*eing everyone's friend sucks donkey balls.

I thought about it as I twirled the ends of my black hair around my fingers and stared up at the ceiling. The bed I was lying on suddenly dipped, pulling me from my thoughts and causing me to flinch at the disruption of my peace and quiet. I glanced at my best friend, who had one hand on her bed to balance herself while she put on her high heels with the other.

Bronagh Murphy was my opposite in every way. When she wasn't pretending she was invisible—she was loud, sassy, and had a solid backbone. She was funny too, and though she didn't think so, she had a *banging* body.

My and Bronagh's pairing was an odd one, and we hadn't always been friends. In fact, it was only over the past few weeks that we decided to give the friendship thing a real go after I was attacked by the school bully, and Bronagh defended me. After that, we quickly found we were, in fact, BFFs and just *had* to hang out all the time.

We were a work in progress for Bronagh, though. I wasn't exactly a social butterfly, I could make friends easily enough when I wanted to, but Bronagh couldn't. She had trust issues, and landing a spot as her friend was a miracle in its own right. I had been in her class for all of secondary school and often saw her around primary school, but I never really knew her. No one did... until Dominic and Damien Slater moved to our town, got lumped into our tutor class and, quite literally, cornered her until she had no choice but to come out swinging.

Damien Slater, my mind drifted. *Where do I start with Damien Slater?*

I licked my lips and exhaled.

Damien was... my God—he was perfect. He was drop-dead gorgeous, tall, had an accent, *and* he made me laugh. He was an identical twin, but to me, he was nothing like his brother Dominic. I knew from the moment I saw him on his first day in school a few months ago that I would secretly obsess over him. I just didn't know I'd be obsessing twenty-four-bloody-seven over him.

I had never had a *real* crush on a boy before Damien entered my life. I thought some boys around school and town were cute, and hot celebrities *obviously* drew my attention like any other red-blooded teenage girl, but I had no one who I really fancied myself being with. That all changed when I first saw Damien. His personality was larger than life, and as cheesy as it sounds, he looked like he was carved by angels. He was one of those perfect people you looked at and instantly knew that they would never glance in your direction, much less gaze in it.

Ten seconds after I clapped eyes on him, I was imagining our wedding. My stomach somersaulted when I pictured his white blond hair standing out against his black tuxedo as we said 'I do'. How his grey eyes would stare into mine as he declared his undying love for me to the world. How his plump rosy lips would feel like velvet as they covered mine and claimed them in a heated kiss. How his smile would erase my every worry and fear and replace it with hope. How his large hands would hold mine when we strolled down the street.

It took another ten seconds for me to realise that I never stood a damn chance. Nearly every girl in our class, and the damn school, most likely had the same thoughts as I did and jumped to be the first one to grab and hold his attention.

It was mortifying to admit it to myself, but Damien consumed a huge part of my life, and we were *barely* even friends. If that didn't label me as pathetic, then I didn't know what would. The only thing on my side was that no one knew those embarrassing pieces of information... except for Bronagh, who was too attentive for her own good.

"Alannah, what're you sighin' for?" she asked, bumping my leg with hers.

I turned my attention to her. "Huh?"

"You keep sighin'."

I do?

"Sorry, I'm just thinkin'."

Bronagh stared at me, a perfectly shaped brow raised in question.

"About Damien?" she asked.

I felt my cheeks stain with heat. Bronagh was my best friend, but that title was new, and that meant she didn't really know the depth of my feelings for Damien. No one did, and if I had it my way, no one would.

"Yeah," I mumbled.

Bronagh simpered. "You're so cute when you blush."

'Cause that's what every eighteen-year-old wants to be viewed as. Cute.

I playfully kicked at her. "Leave me alone."

"Sorry," she said, amusement gleaming in her eyes. "I forget how... much of an introvert you are."

"I'm *so* not an introvert. You are."

"Me?" Bronagh gleefully laughed.

I nodded. "Which one of us kept to 'erself for *years*?"

"I was *purposely* blockin' everyone out, though; you weren't."

I didn't reply, so Bronagh raised her brow and stared at me, a knowing grin on her pink lips.

"Fine," I grumbled. "I'm a *little bit* of an introvert, but it suits me fine. When I try to be outgoin', it fails, so keepin' to one's self is a safe bet."

"When did it fail?" Bronagh quizzed.

When *hadn't* it failed was the real question.

I blinked. "With Damien."

My friend frowned. "You're his friend, his *only* female friend apart from me, and that's only because I'm datin' his brother. If I wasn't, he'd probably try to hit on me then never talk to me again when he realised I wasn't interested."

"It's not like we're even real friends, though. I only see 'im outside of school because I'm with you all the time now, and that means I'm also with Dominic, and where there is Dominic, there is Damien."

"Alannah—"

"I don't like when he flirts with me because I know what he wants," I cut Bronagh off, swallowing. "He is so open about not wantin' a relationship longer than a rumble under the bed sheets, but I don't want to *just* have sex with 'im. I don't want to be on his hit list. I really like 'im, and it sucks that he doesn't like me in the same way."

Bronagh reached over and placed her hand on my knee.

"Sorry, Lana. I wish he was different."

"He is great the way he is," I stressed. "But I want 'im to like *me*. I don't want to be like Destiny or Lexi; they go through lads like it's no one's business, and I can't be like that. I can't be like them just to have his attention. I just... I just wish I was worth more to 'im than a quick shag... you know?"

Bronagh nodded. "Yeah, I know."

The mood had quickly turned depressing, and I felt bad.

"I'm sorry, Bee. I'm bummin' you out on your big night."

She tilted her head. "Me big night?"

I deadpanned. "Your hoo-ha has been deflowered. That means it's a *big* night."

Bronagh widened her eyes before she grabbed a pillow and hit me with it, causing me to sputter with laughter. She hit me with it again, so I squealed and laughed harder.

"You're a bitch," she stated.

I smiled wide. "You love me, though."

"Yeah," Bronagh said, sounding like she just came to some sort of revelation. "I do."

I knew that her accepting me as a friend was a big deal for her, but I knew caring for me was an even bigger deal.

"Hey," I said, gaining her full attention. "I love you too, and that means you're stuck with me for life. Dominic will have to get used to me as a third wheel."

My friend snorted. "He thinks you've a great rack and arse, so he won't mind."

I gasped. "He does *not*!"

"He does," Bronagh tittered. "We randomly talked about it. I'm *totally* cool with you knowin' it too because I know you're the only girl at school who prefers Damien over 'im."

That was the truth.

I cringed. "Mate, Dominic is... *ew*."

Bronagh cracked up with laughter. "Damien is his *identical twin*. They literally have the same everythin'. Well, not the same hair colour, but everythin' else is the same."

I disagreed.

"When I look at them, I see two completely different people. It's hard to explain, but they're nothin' alike to me even though they have the same everythin'. Do you see Damien in Dominic?"

Bronagh shook her head. "At first I did, but now, I don't. Dominic has so much personality that his body can't contain it."

"Speakin' of loverboy." I grinned. "Did it, you know, hurt?"

Bronagh's cheeks tinged with redness as she nodded. "At first, it hurt then it was uncomfortable, and then everythin' changed, and it was amazin'. It honestly wasn't as bad as I always thought it would be, but if Dominic wasn't so focused on makin' me feel good, I think it just would have been sore and nothin' special like most people's first time."

I exhaled. "That's good to know. Maybe I won't be so wound up when I finally lose me own V-card."

"I'm a little sore *now*, but Dominic says that's normal because it was me first time. Eventually, it won't feel uncomfortable at all afterwards. So he says anyway."

I gnawed on my lower lip. "You'd better go on the pill, just to be safe."

"Yeah, Branna said she'd take me to the doctors to get a monthly prescription."

I suddenly giggled. "You're a total slag, needin' the pill and an *actual* condom supply."

Bronagh's face flared with heat once more, and I momentarily wondered if the colour would ever leave her cheeks.

"Stop it. I get so embarrassed when I think of it. And I'm mortified to be on me own with Dominic again."

Come again?

I raised a brow. "But he is your *lad*."

"So?" my friend questioned. "I love 'im, and we're in a relationship, but he just saw me *naked* and took me *virginity*. I can't help but be embarrassed."

"You're so weird," I mused.

Bronagh snorted. "That's not new information."

Male laughter from downstairs got my attention, and I quietened down.

"The twins' brothers," I said upon hearing them, "are *a lot* hotter than what you said they were."

"They are?"

I stared at her as if she had grown an extra head.

"You said they were good lookin', but babe, they're on *fire*. I've never met men quite like Ryder and Kane before. And Alec? That is too much sexiness to claim one person. Then there are the twins, who are another kind of hot. Their gene pool is bloody amazin'.'"

Bronagh bobbed her head in agreement. "You should have seen me when I first met them. I stared without blinkin', and I think I even drooled."

"No one would blame if you did," I commented.

My friend laughed. "Are you ready to go?"

I sighed as I pushed myself from the bed and got to my feet. I straightened out my dress, hoping it wasn't creased.

"I'm as ready as I'll ever be."

Bronagh frowned. "If you'd rather stay—"

"No, I want to go out. I've never been clubbin' before, it's just... I hope I don't get upset if Damien pulls a girl. I have no claim on 'im, but I really like 'im, so you can guarantee me emotions will kick off if he pulls. I just hope I don't cry."

"You know what?" my friend boasted, sudden confidence filling her tone. "*You* are goin' on the pull tonight. You're goin' to kiss the socks off a lad and forget about Damien Slater."

If only.

"Yeah." I whooped with fake enthusiasm. "Good idea."

Bronagh beamed, pleased with herself. "Great. Go on down and tell the lads I'm ready. I'm gonna go get some of Branna's perfume and see if she's ready."

I nodded and left the room. When I reached the ground floor, I turned and walked down the hallway and into the kitchen where I walked headfirst into one of the Slater brothers. I looked up and found Alec Slater looking down at me with a shit-eating grin on his way too perfect face. He placed his large hands on my shoulders to steady me, and he left them there, which had me freaking out because he was too hot for words to be touching me for a long period of time.

"So sorry," I said rapidly.

He continued to grin. "Don't worry your pretty little head, sweetheart."

I heard a groan from inside the kitchen followed by some snickering.

"She just turned eighteen, big brother."

It was Dominic who spoke, and I wanted to pummel him for embarrassing me.

Alec simply winked at me before he removed his hands from my shoulders, moved around me, and ventured off down the hallway then upstairs. I inhaled and exhaled before I stepped into the kitchen. Without realising it, I turned around to the empty space Alec just vacated and stared as if he would magically reappear.

"He's so damn pretty."

I looked to my right when male laughter sounded, and when I found the remaining four Slater brothers staring at me, I widened my eyes.

"Did I say that out loud?" I asked, horrified.

The group nodded, and I felt blood rush up my neck to my cheeks, which prompted me to place my face in my hands.

"You're doing much better than Bronagh if it's any consolation," Dominic offered. "She stared at all my brothers when she first met them. I'm sure she drooled too."

I dropped my hands, my cheeks still aflame.

"Speakin' of Bronagh, go and put 'er out of 'er misery."

Dominic blinked. "You wanna expand on that?"

"She's mortified to see you even though you both... *you know*."

He smirked. "Yeah, *I know*."

Ryder and Kane shook their heads while Damien bumped fists with his twin.

"Go act normal so she can stop freakin' out 'cause when she is freaked, I have to be freaked. Best friend code."

Damien laughed; his brothers didn't. I felt a surge of pleasure that at least *he* thought I was funny.

"I'll go take care of her," Dominic said as he stood up, moved past me, and left the room.

When I was alone with the remaining three brothers, I found

myself moving back and forth on my heels. I stopped moving when fear of my ankles giving way under my high heels entered my mind.

"So." I cleared my throat. "You're American."

Alannah, oh my God.

I cringed at the shocking conversation starter.

"And you're Irish," Kane rumbled. "Now that we've gotten the obvious out of the way, how close are you with Bronagh?"

I wasn't prepared for the question, nor the tension in Kane's tone and the accusation in his glaring eyes.

"Bro," Damien began, but one look from his older brother silenced him.

Kane looked back at me, awaiting my reply, and I could do nothing but stare at him. He was extremely intimidating. Bronagh warned me about his appearance, and I knew that his scars wouldn't bother me because his looks didn't define him, but she failed to mention that he was a bit of an arse.

"Close as new friends can be, I guess," I replied with a one shoulder shrug.

Kane cocked a brow. "Has she talked to you about us?"

"Us?"

"Me. My brothers."

I blinked. "Um, no. She told me your names, that you're from New York and said you're all good lookin', but that's about it."

Ryder smiled and was about to speak, but Kane wasn't finished.

"Are you *gonna* ask questions about us?"

I got the feeling he didn't like me, though I wasn't sure why because he didn't know me.

I swallowed. "No, why would I?"

"Because you're curious."

"About Damien, not you."

I realised what I said the second the words left my mouth, and I wanted the ground to open up and swallow me whole because it sounded sassy, and I was rarely sassy.

"I didn't mean that like it sounded," I blurted. "I mean—"

"I know what you mean," Kane cut me off, leaning back in his chair as he eyed me up and down. "You aren't the first girl to be curious about him, and you won't be the last."

What is happening?

"Ryder," Damien grunted. "Do something."

Ryder gave him a slight shake of his head and remained quiet.

"I'm sorry, but have I done somethin' wrong on you?" I asked Kane, hating how uncomfortable he had made me feel. "Because if I haven't, I want to know what the hell your problem is and why I'm bein' interrogated for no bloody reason."

Kane raised his brows, Ryder smiled, and Damien choked on air.

"I'm just getting a feel for you," Kane replied, his eyes still locked on mine.

I honestly thought my heart was going to explode from apprehension, but I stood my ground.

"Well, you can do it in a polite way without the attitude. Introducin' yourself and simply being nice is a good way to start. I don't know what Bronagh has said about me, but I'm a nice person who can only take so much bullshit. If you don't have anythin' nice to say to me, don't say it at all. I'll be more than happy to ignore you."

"Well, fuck me," Kane said then Ryder burst out laughing.

Meanwhile, I was busy trying to control my breathing and praying I didn't pass out. I didn't do confrontation, and somehow, that was just what I was involved in… and I think I won.

"I think this conversation is over," I said and left the room in a hurry.

"Thanks a lot, asshole!" Damien snapped.

The laughter continued as I heard a chair scrape across the floor, footsteps beat against the ground, and a presence come up behind me. I turned around just as Damien reached for me. His hand, that I'm sure was intended for my shoulder, latched onto my right breast and shock froze me to the spot.

"I did *not* mean to tit grab," Damien said, his eyes on mine, but his hand remained on my breast.

My pulse sped up.

"It's… okay," I squeaked.

I looked down at Damien's hand, and when he realised he was still holding my breast, he dropped his hand like it was on fire.

"Shit," he said, flustered. "I wanted to apologise for Kane's behaviour, *not* grope you."

I was so embarrassed that I considered walking out of the house without further words exchanged, but I didn't. Instead, I swallowed and forced a tight-lipped smile.

"It's whatever; he was probably just messin' with me."

"Yeah," Damien lied.

We both knew Kane wasn't playing with me.

"Forget him," Damien continued.

Kane Slater wasn't someone you easily forgot.

"Already forgotten," I said, my forced smile still in place.

Damien stared through my smile. I knew he did because his face softened. He took a step towards me and opened his mouth to speak but was interrupted when Alec jogged down the stairs. I took a step back and nodded at Alec, who moved past us with just a wink shot in our direction. Damien looked over his shoulder when Alec spoke, and his other brothers laughed. The three of them then walked out of the kitchen, and Alec was boasting.

"All I'm saying is little brother has skills that he *obviously* picked up from me. His girl called out to God more times than I could count. He was in control of that puss—"

"Finish that sentence, you slapper, and I will end you!" Bronagh snarled as she descended the stairs with Dominic and Branna in tow.

Alec made the motion of sealing his lips, though I doubt he was finished with teasing her and Dominic about their special night. I wanted to tell him to leave her alone, but I was still pretty shocked over Kane pulling a fast one on me and treating me like I was doing something wrong.

Damien stepped away from me without a word when Bronagh

came to my side and took hold of my hand. I smiled at her and gave her hand a reassuring squeeze.

"Are you ready?" she rhetorically asked.

I exhaled a deep breath as we walked out of her house and into the night.

As I'll ever be.

"I should have stayed at home," Bronagh yawned and stretched.

Two hours ago, I would have jumped at the chance to chill in her room and watch a film, but now that I was tipsy and actually feeling the music in the club, I wasn't letting Bronagh get comfortable enough in case she *did* fall asleep and had to be brought home.

"Have a drink and loosen up." I cheered, tipping my vodka and Coke in her direction. "This is fun!"

Bronagh shot me a look that would silence many people but not me.

"We have school in the mornin', so I'm passin' on havin' a drink," she said with a raised brow. "You should just stop altogether. Otherwise, you're goin' to be dyin' with a hangover when you wake up."

I didn't want to be reminded of school, or anything outside of having adult fun. This was my very first time being in a club and drinking alcohol. We would be finished school in mere months and I knew both Bronagh and I would do well on our Leaving Certificate exams so we didn't have to worry about them. The chances of me frequently letting loose like this were slim to none so I wanted to *enjoy* it.

I blew her a kiss. "Thanks, Ma, I'll keep that in mind."

"Bitch!" she stated, making me laugh and her grin.

I glanced to my left and saw Branna on Ryder's lap and they were so completely wrapped up in each other that they didn't notice anyone around them. Alec, Damien, and Dominic were off somewhere in the club, and Kane was still seated next to Bronagh. We hadn't spoken since he apologised to me upon entering the club, and I was happy enough to leave it at that for the night. He looked just as done as Bronagh with the club scene, and it was obvious he hated being surrounded by so many people, but I wasn't letting his chilled demeanour rub off on me *or* Bronagh.

"Let's dance," I shouted to my friend.

I laughed because I practically felt her sigh even though I couldn't hear it.

"Don't even think about sayin' no, Bronagh," I warned. "We have to bond, and dancin' helps with that so *come on*."

My friend groaned, and I feared she wasn't going to budge, so I used the only weapon I had in my arsenal. My eyes. My father had always told me that my eyes would be the death of him because they were big, brown, and as dangerous as a puppy's. I gave Bronagh my best pleading look, and before she even verbally agreed to dance with me, I saw her cave, so I held my hand out to her.

"Okay," she groaned and grabbed my hand.

Game, set, match.

"Yay," I beamed.

Bronagh playfully rolled her eyes.

"We will be back later," I said to the table without looking at anyone in particular.

Bronagh looked back at Kane, Branna and Ryder when they gave us their attention.

"By later," she said, "she hopefully means after the *next* song."

I burst into laughter, earning a big smile from Bronagh.

"Fat chance of that." I devilishly smiled. "Now, come on; I *love* this song!"

I couldn't tell what song was playing, but I knew the beat, and that was enough to get me excited. I danced with Bronagh until my thighs and calves burned from overuse. I laughed until my throat hurt, and I tossed back drinks like it was no one's business. I wanted to tell Bronagh how much fun I was having, but then I felt a hand on my forearm lead me to the middle of the crowd.

"Hey," I shouted and tugged my arm. "Let go."

I looked up at the owner of the hand that had hold of me, and when grey eyes and a mop of white hair became clear through my slightly drunken gaze, I beamed.

"Damien!"

I focused on him and found he was smiling down at me, his eyes gleaming with amusement. He placed his hands on my waist, and without a word, he tugged my body until I was flush against him, and it took my breath away. When I gathered my bearings, I placed my hands on his shoulders and bit my lip when I rolled my body against his. I practically felt his moan as his hands on my waist squeezed my flesh.

He said something to me. I saw his lips move, but I couldn't hear him. I got on my tiptoes and shouted, "I can't hear you."

He grabbed my hand and led me off the dance floor. When he turned to face me, I had no idea what possessed me to do it, but I leaned up, placed my hands on either side of his face, and moved in, pressing my lips against his. Damien froze for a couple of seconds then he eagerly responded to my kiss. He wrapped his arms around my body and pulled my body as close as he could get me.

"Alannah," I felt him say against my lips.

I pulled back from our kiss feeling breathless, giddy with excitement, and hot to the core.

"That was amazin'," I exhaled.

Damien squinted down at me before he grabbed my hand once more and led us over to two huge men that stood outside a door. I avoided looking at both men because they were intimidating. Instead, I silently followed Damien when the men parted and opened the door they seemed to be guarding. When we stepped into the corridor, and the door behind us was closed, a veil of silence fell. I looked over my shoulder, surprised that I couldn't hear a single sound from the club.

"Me ears are ringin'," I shouted before I remembered I didn't have to.

Damien looked at me and chuckled, then silently led me down the corridor and through the last door. When we stepped into a huge living area, the first thing I spotted was the big ass bed. My first reaction upon seeing it should have been uncertainty, but a devilish streak struck me at that moment and pushed my legs to move toward the bed. When my knees knocked against it, I bent forward and ran my hand over the linen.

Silk.

"This feels so good," I hummed.

I heard a sharp intake of breath, and a rush of pleasure shot through me. I knew my dress had hiked up a little bit more than what was decent, and I knew in my bones that Damien could see everything on display.

"Heaven help me."

I stood up straight, and without fixing my dress, I turned around.

"Did you say somethin'?" I questioned.

Damien lifted his arm and ran his hand through his hair, and I realised it was an action I desperately wanted to do.

"I said," he rumbled. "Heaven help me."

"Why do you need help?" I asked. "You aren't in trouble."

"On the contrary." Damien smirked. "I think I'm in a whole heap of trouble."

I swallowed. "What trouble would that be?"

"The five-foot-five, black hair, and brown eyes kind."

Butterflies exploded in my belly.

"You think I'm trouble?"

"Babe," Damien chuckled. "I think you're the definition of it."

How could that be?

"I think you've got me confused with someone else," I said, falling into a sitting position on the bed when I tried to take a step back. "I've never been in trouble in me life."

"No, I'm sure you haven't," Damien agreed. "But I think you could stir up a lot of it."

"Yeah," I asked. "Like what?"

"Like how one kiss has me wanting to touch you in ways you've never been touched."

My heart slammed into my chest.

"Ho-how do you know what ways I've been touched?" I stammered. "I could have already been touched in every way possible."

"*Babe*," was all he said as his cheeks dimpled.

I felt a blush burn up my neck, and he acknowledged my virginity with one word and a damn smirk.

"Fine." I licked my lips. "No one else has touched me, but *I've* touched me an awful lot."

The look of desire that Damien shot my way sent shivers up my spine.

I swallowed. "Why don't you change the former and touch me?"

Damien's face lost all traces of amusement.

"Be careful, Freckles," he warned. "I think we should just cool it and talk—"

"I don't want to talk." I cut him off. "I want to kiss you, to touch you… I want… I want to get into trouble with you."

"My *God*." He groaned and put his face in his hands. "You aren't a sex only girl, Lana. You're the flowers, chocolate, cuddle nights in, and steady boyfriend kind of girl. And I love that about you, but I can't give you that."

I frowned.

"Don't look at me like that," Damien said, looking flustered. "I'm trying to do right by you. I'm trying to convince myself that you don't really want me like this—"

"I do." I cut him off once more. "I know your situation, and I'm not a fool. I know it's just sex with you, but I want you so much that I'll take it."

I recalled my earlier conversation with Bronagh. I said I didn't want Damien to want me just for sex, that I didn't want to be on his hit list, but I had a strong feeling that I needed to experience him in any capacity.

"This was a bad idea. I shouldn't have brought you in here." He began to pace. "I just wanted to talk to you, but *damn*, you look edible, and you smell and taste so good, it's all I can do to stay on this side of the room."

"Come to me," I beckoned. "Don't think about the after, think about now. If I'm angry later, it's on me. This is probably a stupid idea, but I've never needed someone like I need you. If this is a mistake, let me make it and learn from it."

"You've been drinking," Damien said flatly.

"I've sobered up a hell of a lot since you told me I was trouble."

"You *are* trouble."

"Prove it," I challenged.

Damien took a step forward then hesitated before he said, "Let's just chill and talk for a while. Just… just to see if this is what you really want."

The words were hardly out of his mouth before I turned and scrambled up the bed, flopping onto my back.

"What are you doing?"

"What do you mean?" I asked, holding my position. "I'm chillin'."

Damien folded his arms across his chest, the corners of his lips twitching.

"You usually chill on a bed with your thighs parted?" he asked, a slight hint of laughter in his tone.

"Actually," I said, "this is how I lie on me bed. It's kind of… freein'."

Damien dropped his gaze from my eyes to my parted thighs. I saw his Adam's apple bob as he swallowed. He quickly crossed the room, turned his back to me, and sat on the edge of the bed. Without turning around, he patted the spot next to him and said, "Come here and talk with me. I want to hear your voice."

I practically floated to his side, and it made Damien laugh.

"What do you want me to say?" I said, a little breathless.

Damien turned his gaze on me, and as he looked into my eyes, he said, "Say anything. I just want to hear your voice. I love your voice."

I felt as if the air had been sucked from the room.

"You do?" I rasped.

Damien licked his lips. "Yeah, I hear your voice even when you aren't around."

My heart slammed against my chest.

"You do?" I repeatedly nodded.

"I hear you when it's quiet," he said, dropping his gaze to my lips.

I lazily dragged my tongue across my lower lip.

"What do I say when you hear me voice?" I asked; my voice sounded thick with desire.

Damien huffed a laugh. "You don't want to know, Freckles."

I scrunched up my face in displeasure. "Why do you call me that?"

He lifted his hand, and with his pinkie finger, he ran the tip over my nose and underneath my eyes.

"You have a splash of freckles right here," he murmured.

I frowned. "If you say you think they're cute, I may slap you."

Damien simpered. "Cute is not a word I associate with you."

My pulse spiked.

"What word do you associate with me?"

"I have a few," he replied, lowering his hand from my face. "Smart, funny, hard-working... beautiful, elegant, sexy as sin."

I gasped. "You think I'm funny?"

Damien almost instantly burst into laughter.

"Hell yes, you're funny." He chortled. "Out of all the words I said, you picked funny."

I blushed. "No one has ever said I was funny before."

"Well, you are."

I leaned in a little closer to him. "You think I'm beautiful and elegant?"

"And sexy as sin," he breathed. "Can't forget about that."

I smiled, and I heard a little groan come up Damien's throat like he was straining to contain it. I stood up from the bed and kicked my heels off before I turned to face him. I stared down at Damien, and he stared up at me.

I couldn't stand it anymore.

My body felt like it was a live wire of electricity. I wanted Damien to kiss me and touch me more than my next breath. I didn't want him to make the first move; I was too aware of him to allow that to happen. Instead, I stepped forward, parted his thighs with my knees, and stepped between them.

"Alannah, what are—"

I brought my mouth down on top of his and took what I'd wanted since the first moment I saw him. I lifted my hands, thrusting them into his hair, and almost dropped to my knees. His hair was thick and soft—so freaking soft. I tangled my fingers around the strands and tugged.

"You're playing a dangerous game with me, Lana," Damien said against my lips, his voice husky. "I'd walk away if I were you."

Boldness surged through me.

"That sounds like a challenge to me."

"Talking," Damien groaned into my mouth. "We're supposed to be talking."

"We are," I replied, sliding my tongue over his lower lip. "We're talkin' with our bodies."

Damien broke our kiss and stared up at me, his expression one of shock. It was quickly replaced by one so full of heat and longing that by the time he drew me against him, I was shaking.

"I want you so much," he breathed. "God knows I've dreamed of touching you, kissing you, tasting you."

I had to lock my knees together to keep from falling to them.

"What will you do to me if I let you touch me?" I asked, my voice thick with desire.

"I'd kiss you. Nice and slow until my lips are all you know. My hands would explore every inch of you until you only knew my touch. I'd love you so good the feel of me will be imbedded into you for life. I'd make your body *mine*."

"Yes," I said, breathlessly. "Please, I want that."

More than my next breath.

Damien pulled me against him, and covered his mouth with mine. He growled against my lips before he stood up. Hooking his arms around my thighs, he picked me up as he moved. I gasped into his mouth, latching my arms around his neck and wrapping my legs around his waist.

"I love how tall you are," I panted, pulling back to gaze at him. "It makes me feel tiny."

"You *are* tiny," Damien said, pushing my dress up with one hand so he could palm my behind.

He touched his lips to mine once more, moulding them together as his tongue slid inside in a kiss so ravenous it caused my knees to shake, my heart to slam into my chest and my skin to flush with pleasure. My thoughts were scattered with every thrust and slide of his tongue licking against my own. Damien's kiss was so consuming I didn't know where he started and I ended.

"You're so gorgeous," I blurted against his lips. "And I love your hair. It's so freakin' pretty and soft. What conditioner do you use? Actually, never mind. I love your face. My *God*, do I love your face."

I felt Damien's laughter vibrate against my lips before he kissed down my jawline to my neck where he placed feathered kisses over my skin.

"You wouldn't *believe* the things I've dreamed of doin' to you and you doin' to me," I purred, hoping to God I sounded sultry.

Damien scraped his teeth over my sweet spot, and it caused my back to arch, which pushed my breasts against him. His hands on my behind squeezed me tightly.

"Why don't you tell me in detail what you dreamed of us doing," he asked, his voice raspy.

"You'd used your mo-mouth on me," I stammered. "And when I thought that would kill me, you'd add in your fingers."

Damien lightly bit my neck, encouraging me to continue.

"Your tongue." I squealed. "You'd taste me all over."

I gasped when Damien suddenly turned and dislodged my arms and legs from around him as he pushed me from his body and onto the bed with a bounce. He rid himself of his shirt with one tug and watching that sent a shiver up my spine.

"You're perfect," I said, staring up at him.

His tanned skin seemed to glow in the lightening as strands of his hair fell forward into his eyes. He lifted a hand to push them away, and the flex of his bicep had my insides clenching with need. His broad shoulders were begging for my teeth to sink into them, and the lines of his abdominal muscles taunted my fingers to run over them.

You have no idea what you're doing to me.

"That'd be you, baby," he said as he gripped the hem of my dress and pushed it up to my waist.

Without a single word he gripped the top of my dress, pulled the straps down my shoulders and tugged the material down until my bare breasts were free. I didn't wear a bra with my dress, I didn't need to, and it seemed like Damien appreciated it if his groan was anything to go by. He left my dressed bunched up at my waist and leaned back on his heels so he could roam his eyes over me.

"You're stunning, Lana."

My body hummed with delight at his words and at his hands when he slid them up my thighs, skimmed my stomach, and flattened them over my breasts. He cupped them, giving them a gentle squeeze before he ran his thumbs over the sensitive pink tips. The tingling sensation drew a slight moan from me as heat pooled between my legs, an incessant throb growing with each tantalizing touch.

I felt my cheeks burn when his gaze locked on the centre of my thighs.

"Lace?" he questioned without looking at me.

"I like pretty un-underwear."

"So do I." Damien looked up at me with fire in his eyes.

"What are you goin' to do to me?" I asked, my voice barely a whisper.

He licked his lips. "What I've wanted to do to you from the first moment I saw you."

I blinked. "What's that?"

I shrieked when he gripped the hem of my underwear and yanked them from my body. If the sound of fabric tearing was anything to go by, I'd say he even partially ripped them in the process. I could barely breathe when my thighs were parted and Damien brought his face down to my pussy.

He inhaled, and I knew mortification at that moment.

"Damien!" I cried and desperately tried to shut my legs. "Why are you sniffin' me? Oh, God! Do you have a weird fetish or somethin'?"

He laughed but didn't move a muscle other than when he stopped me from wriggling.

"No," he mused. "I'm savouring how you smell because it's damn good."

If I ever spoke to him again after this, it would be too soon.

"This is indecent!" I stated, my entire face burning. "You can't just—Damien!"

The flick of his hot wet tongue was unexpected and oh so delicious.

"Holy Mary Mother of God." I exhaled.

"Pray to whoever you want, Freckles. No one can save you from me now."

With that said, he began to lick and suck on my pussy lips then he used his tongue to part them. I felt myself go cross-eyed, and it was all I could do not to buck my hips in his face. His tongue slid up the trail of slick heat until he curled it around my clit and gifted me with a sensation I never knew existed.

I reached down with my hand, tangled my fingers in his hair, and held on for dear life.

He applied pressure as he swirled his tongue around the sensitive bud, and the action sucked the air out of me. It was too much sensation—too much of a new sensation—for my body to handle. I couldn't lie still, so Damien hooked his arms around my thighs and applied heavy-handed pressure on them, which helped to keep me in place.

"Dame." I panted as my breathing turned irregular.

His response was to rapidly shake his head from side to side, flicking his tongue over my clit as he moved, sending shocks of bliss shooting up my spine.

"Oh God," I shouted at the new sensation it brought. "Oh God, oh God, oh *God*!"

I screamed for only a second before I sucked in air, holding it in my lungs as mounting pleasure suddenly caused my thighs to quiver with anticipation. For a second, I felt a sharp pain then numbness before a thrashing of what I could only describe as Heaven washed over me. The throbbing of delight exploded through me. My muscles contracted in response as if they were cheering on the sensation that curled around them.

I released the breath I was holding when my lungs demanded I do so. I didn't even realise that I had closed my eyes, but I couldn't open them if I wanted to, so it didn't even matter. My limbs became lax as all traces of energy fled, and it was all I could do not to fall to sleep.

"You're so beautiful, Freckles," Damien's voice rasped as he parted my thighs farther apart. "I'm sorry if this hurts."

That was the only warning he gave me before my insides screamed as they were stretched and invaded. My eyes flew open, and a strangled whimper passed my lips. My hands latched onto Damien's thick arms as he stilled inside me, and my back arched as a pinch of pain cut through my core.

"It'll pass," Damien whispered, his voice hoarse.

He lowered his head and kissed me with so much tenderness and care it was easy to focus on his lips instead of the pain. He whispered words of encouragement against my swollen lips, and brushed the tip of his nose my cheek before he rested his forehead on mine and stared deeply into my eyes.

We were one in that moment.

Before long, I wriggled my hips, pulling a pained groan from Damien who was trying his hardest to remain as still as a statue. I wriggled once more and only felt a slight bit of discomfort, but to my surprise, the stinging pain had subsided completely. The second I hummed, Damien took it as a green light to move. When he withdrew slowly and thrust back in, my muscles tightened.

It didn't hurt, but it didn't exactly feel good either.

"Relax, baby," he rasped. "You're squeezing me like a vice."

"*You* relax!" I countered. "It feels like a melon is bein' shoved up me."

Damien had the nerve to chuckle, and it held my attention, but when he withdrew and thrust back into my body, I allowed my head to fall back against the bed as I moaned. He fell into a rhythm, and it took away my ability to think coherently, let alone speak.

"Christ," Damien breathed as he lowered his head and planted kisses along my neck. "You feel incredible."

I lifted my legs and wrapped them around his hips, hooking my ankles over the other to lock them in place. I couldn't control how vocal I was, especially when every thrust sent a ripple of shivers over my body and made me hunger for more.

"Oh!" I gasped when a lick of pleasure curled around my inner muscles.

"Yeah," Damien rasped. "*Oh!*"

"Keep doin' that," I panted. "Oh, keep doin' *that*!"

"I couldn't stop if you paid me," Damien replied, sweat beading on his forehead.

Fast and hard poundings replaced the slow and gentle thrusts. I dug my fingers into Damien's flesh when the desire to bite something struck. I tried to hold back, but I couldn't. Like an animal I leaned forward, and latched my teeth onto his neck and bit down.

Damien thrust into me so hard in response a resounding *slap* echoed the room.

"You're going to ruin me for any other woman."

I damn well hoped so.

"God, I could keep you forever," he proceeded to say, his voice thick with passion.

I released him, and pressed my forehead to his as I swallowed. "Will you keep me?"

"Yes," he panted, nudging my face with his. "God, yes. You're mine."

My heart thumped with delight, and a huge smile overtook my face. It was quickly wiped away when scorching heat spread over my body like butter, causing goose bumps to break out on my skin. My mouth suddenly opened in a silent scream when a rumble started in my core and kept building until an explosion of light burst from within me. The pleasure that began to ripple through my body sent small spasms rolling through my limbs and left me trembling.

When I came to, I was repeating Damien's name.

"Yes, yes," he panted as my inner walls clenched around him.

"You promise to keep me?" I asked as he pumped into me harder, faster, deeper.

"Yes," he almost shouted. "I promise. *Lana!*"

His movements became frantic then, and just as his thrusts slowed and turned to twitches, I watched the sensations he experienced as they took over his body and played out like a film on his handsome face.

His eyes closed, he bit down on his lower lip, his cheeks flushed a pretty shade of pink, his brows furrowed, and his muscles tensed. Ten or so seconds later, it was like every ounce of tension that had worked its way onto his face melted away and spread over his body like a deep tissue massage.

It was the only warning I got before he fell forward.

"Damien!" I laughed as the air was knocked out of me.

All of his weight was on me, and while I loved it, it was too much for my chest to handle. I nudged him, and he groaned as he used his elbows to prop himself up, taking most of his weight off me.

"Hi." I smiled up at him.

My mind, body, and heart were so content and blissful that nothing could have ruined the moment.

"I didn't mean to say that," Damien said, his eyes flashing with... terror.

Except that.

I blinked. "Say what?"

"That stuff," he said, clearing his throat. "About keeping you."

A feeling of sickness began to form in the pit of my stomach.

"Damien," I whispered. "Can you not say that while you're still *inside* me?"

He looked down at our still connected bodies and quickly pulled out of me. I winced, and he apologised. I was lying on the bed sheets, so I had nothing to cover myself with except my hands. Damien disposed of the now used condom—a condom I didn't even know he had put on—and began to dress at a shocking speed. I began to panic and felt like I should do the same, so I joined him in fixing my dress until we were dressed and looking as we did when we entered the room—just a little less put together.

"I don't understand what is happenin'," I said as I slid my feet back into my shoes, my feet screaming in protest.

"I shouldn't have said that shit."

Striking me would have hurt less.

I flinched. "Don't say that."

"I have to; otherwise, you'll believe it."

"So I'm not to believe that you said you'd keep me?" I demanded. "That you *promised* to? What the hell did you say it for then?"

"Alannah, I'd have agreed to a sex change operation at that point of sex," he said flatly. "I couldn't help it. My mind and body were both focused on the sensation, and my voice took on a role of its own."

I felt like I was going to throw up.

"You're ruinin' this!" I said, my lower lip wobbling. "You're ruinin' everythin' about me first time. Why are you doin' this to me?"

Damien's face blanched. "I'm sorry, but I won't lie to you."

"What's the lie?"

"When I promised to keep you," he stated.

I felt my eyes well with tears.

"Damien," I whispered.

"It's not that I *can't* keep you, Lana; it's that I don't *want* to."

He couldn't look me in the eyes as he spoke the words that I knew I'd never forget. The force of it had me stumbling back a few steps as if he'd struck me. I probably had no right to feel betrayed, but I did, and it hurt more than I cared to admit.

"I'm goin' to get cl-cleaned up," I stammered.

"No." Damien frowned. "Please, we have to talk about this. What I mean is—"

"I don't think anythin' you have to say would make me feel better," I cut him off, trying my hardest to keep my emotions in check.

"Alannah—"

"It's fine," I cut him off again.

"It's fucking not," he countered. "I knew this was a bad idea. Just look at how upset you are! This is why I've tried to stay away from you. You're a good girl, and I knew you'd let your emotions take centre stage. This was a mistake!"

His words were the honest truth, and I think that was why they pained me so much.

"You were right. This was a mistake, but I've made it." I swallowed. "And I'll learn from it, too."

Damien reached for me, but I moved farther away from him and headed towards the connecting room that I assumed was a bathroom.

"I don't want to speak to you anymore, Damien," I said as I opened the door.

I never wanted to speak to him again.

"Lana," was all he said.

"Alannah," I said, my hold on the door handle tightening. "Me name is *Alannah*."

I entered the bathroom, closed the door behind me, and locked it. Aimlessly, I relieved myself and cleaned up as best as I could with small pieces of tissue paper. Instead of leaving the bathroom, I leaned my back against the wall and slid down it until my behind hit the floor.

I wasn't sure how long I sat there, but it was long enough for the tears that flowed from my eyes and splashed onto my cheeks to dry. Between my thighs felt strange—like a sweet tenderness that I couldn't shake. I thought I heard raised voices, and when I heard a knock on the door, I flinched.

"Lana?" I heard my name being softly spoken. "It's me; can I come in?"

Bronagh.

I stood up, moved over to the door, unlocked it, and then sat on the closed lid of the toilet. Bronagh entered the bathroom and quickly locked it behind her. She kicked off her heels, bent down to her knees, and then reached forward and engulfed me into a tight hug. When I put my arms around her, I released a pain laced cry.

At that moment, I was both hurt and mortified. I realised I had thrown myself at Damien like I had no shame, and now, shame was all that filled me. I couldn't begin to form the words to tell Bronagh how forward I behaved out of fear that she would judge me, so I kept my mouth shut.

"It's goin' to be okay, Lana. You're strong and won't let an annoyin' American prick get you down, right?"

I managed a snort as I pulled back from our hug. I grabbed some tissue to wipe up the snot running from my nose. I was a mess, and I knew I looked as bad as I felt.

"You know somethin'?" I sniffled. "I know Nico is your fella, but I thought he was the prick and Damien was the nice one. I was so wrong. Nico is honest and has always been 'imself whether you like 'im or hate 'im. Damien, though... He is like a snake in human form. I hate 'im."

I couldn't fault Damien for being upfront before we had sex, but the lies he spewed during it and the bullshit excuse he had for saying them angered me.

"If it makes you feel better," Bronagh interjected, "Dominic really *is* a prick."

I started laughing through my tears. I frowned when Bronagh sat down on her behind and winced at the contact. It was a reminder that she was no longer a virgin either, but her first time had been magical, while mine had the magic sucked from me ten seconds after ending.

"I just realised we both lost our virginity tonight to the twins."

"Well... at least we can be sore and hate 'em together."

I was still upset—that didn't even begin to cover it—but I laughed at Bronagh's joke, and the carefree sound helped a tiny bit. Even with my friend by my side and laughter coming from me, I couldn't help but feel like a layer of stone had just sealed itself over my heart. I would never willingly put myself in a situation where I would feel pain like this again.

Fool me once, shame on you; fool me twice, shame on me.

I called Bronagh's name when the silence that surrounded us was snatched away, and a loud thumping noise could be heard from outside. I didn't know how I knew, but I knew Damien had left the room with the door open and fled down the corridor and back into the club. Getting as far away from me as he possibly could.

The fucking coward.

Bronagh looked at me when I spoke.

"Yeah?"

"Are you ready to go back outside?" I quizzed. "I can hear 'RAMPAGE' bein' cheered now that they've stopped the music for the fight."

Things were a blur of activity as Bronagh jumped to her feet, put her heels back on, and pulled me out of the room and back down the corridor to the club. Bodies of all shapes and sizes crowded around the platform that Dominic and another fighter were on. I couldn't concentrate with the noise and a sea of people, so when Bronagh broke through the crowd to reach Dominic after he won the fight, I stayed long enough to hug when she returned to my side. The second she become solely focused on Dominic, I slipped away from her and headed out of the club.

When I got outside, no one was around, not even the bouncers who had granted us entrance to the club hours before. I was glad to have a moment's solitude so I could try to wrap my head around what happened. I sat on the curb and fought off a fresh batch of tears.

This is a disaster.

There was never going to be a 'Damien and Alannah' in the way I wanted, and he made sure of that. No, *we* made damn sure of that. He took my virginity, but I was the eejit who practically begged him to take it. For that, I had no one to blame but myself… and my god-forsaken hormones.

Damien came into our intimacy with no illusions or lies coated in pretty words—until he got what he wanted. Beforehand, he'd said he didn't want a relationship, he just wanted sex, and for me to feel so broken over him keeping his word was foolish.

In the back of my mind, I'd silently hoped that once we'd had sex, Damien would want to be with me. If *that* wasn't the dumbest misconception that filled the heads of teenage girls across the world, then I didn't know what was.

The pain in my chest was nothing like I had ever felt before, and I didn't know how to deal with it. I needed Bronagh. I needed my friend. I heard a noise behind me, and I wasn't sure why, but because I thought of Bronagh, I assumed it would be her. I wanted to look around, but a sudden case of dizziness struck me, and I had trouble remaining sitting upright. Just when I thought my head and vision was clearing, I felt a knock on the back of my head that was followed by my body falling backwards.

It didn't hurt, and the first thing I thought of was that I was passing out because I had drunk alcohol for the first time. I figured my spike of emotions had pushed my body into stress-out mode, and my mind just switched off as a result. I was glad of it. I was glad when I found myself facing darkness because, at the current moment, darkness was a more welcoming sight than the thought of Damien Slater. I wasn't granted that peace because before I completely shut off, his voice was that last thing that ran through my mind.

It's not that I can't keep you, Lana; it's that I don't want to.

Damien didn't want me, but what hurt the most was that I knew deep down, I'd always want him no matter what. I'd never let him or anyone else know it, though. Damien might have hurt me, but I would *never* give him the opportunity to do it again.

He said he didn't want me, and for as long as I'd live, I'd never forget it.

ABOUT THE AUTHOR

L.A. Casey is a *New York Times* and *USA Today* best-selling author who juggles her time between her mini-me and writing. She was born, raised and currently resides in Dublin, Ireland. She enjoys chatting with her readers, who love her humour and Irish accent as much as her books.

Casey's first book, *DOMINIC*, was independently published in 2014 and became an instant success on Amazon. She is both traditionally and independently published and is represented by Mark Gottlieb from Trident Media Group.

To read more about this author, visit her website at www.lacaseyauthor.com

ACKNOWLEDGEMENTS

I've *finally* reached this section of the book! I've been wanting to write the acknowledgments to *BRANNA* for a very long time. After so many delays with this novella, and hitting so many patches of writer's block, and a never-ending loop of rewrites, I'm delighted to have finished with it, and to be content and happy with it.

It is another book down in the *Slater Brothers* series, and it is surreal to think that I've only got *DAMIEN*, *ALANNAH*, and *BROTHERS* to go. I always thought *DOMINIC* would be a lone novel, and that I'd never get to write the stories of his family and friends, but here I am, eight books later and still going strong.

I have to thank my best friends, Yessi Smith and Mary Johnson, for their constant support with my writing and their treasured friendship. Jill Sava for being the best PA I could have ever asked for—thank you for all you do for me. Jenny from Editing4Indies for taking on the task of cleaning up the manuscript, and Nicola Rhead for taking time out of your busy schedule to polish it off with a proofread. Mayhem Cover Creations for the fabulously stunning cover, and JT formatting for making my words look pretty. Mark Gottlieb for being a kickass agent, and my family for being my biggest cheerleaders.

And last, but never least, my readers. *BRANNA* is for you guys, because God knows you've wanted it to release more than me over these past few months. I love you all dearly, and even though I can't reply to all the Facebook messages, Twitter mentions, and emails you send me, please know that I see them all, and they make my heart happy.

Thank you <3

47870087R00094

Made in the USA
Middletown, DE
04 September 2017